Goddess Girls

PALLAS
THE
PAL

Goddess Girls

PALLAS
THE
PAL

JOAN HOLUB & SUZANNE WILLIAMS

Aladdin

NEW YORK   LONDON   TORONTO   SYDNEY   NEW DELHI

This book is a work of fiction. Any references to historical events, real people, or real places are used fictitiously. Other names, characters, places, and events are products of the author's imagination, and any resemblance to actual events or places or persons, living or dead, is entirely coincidental.

ALADDIN

An imprint of Simon & Schuster Children's Publishing Division

1230 Avenue of the Americas, New York, New York 10020

First Aladdin paperback edition December 2016

Text copyright © 2016 by Joan Holub and Suzanne Williams

Cover illustration copyright © 2016 by Glen Hanson

Also available in an Aladdin hardcover edition.

All rights reserved, including the right of reproduction in whole or in part in any form.

ALADDIN and related logo are registered trademarks of Simon & Schuster, Inc.

For information about special discounts for bulk purchases, please contact Simon & Schuster Special Sales at 1-866-506-1949 or business@simonandschuster.com.

The Simon & Schuster Speakers Bureau can bring authors to your live event. For more information or to book an event, contact the Simon & Schuster Speakers Bureau at 1-866-248-3049 or visit our website at www.simonspeakers.com.

Book designed by Karin Paprocki

The text of this book was set in Baskerville.

Manufactured in the United States of America 1116 OFF

2 4 6 8 10 9 7 5 3 1

Library of Congress Control Number 2016937780

ISBN 978-1-4814-5008-9 (hc)

ISBN 978-1-4814-5007-2 (pbk)

ISBN 978-1-4814-5009-6 (eBook)

We appreciate our Goddess Girls reader pals!

*Emily and Grondine Family, Ariel P., Amelia G., McKay O.,
Reese O., Lillia L., Kira L., Renee G., Haley G., Riley G.,
Gabby G., Katherine Q., Marilyn M., Kathy C., Valerie U.,
Angela L., Bibi L., Ashley J., Trenyce W., Paris O., Olivia C.,
Keny Y., Koko Y., Madison W., Caitlin R., Hannah R.,
Virginia Anna J., Shelby Lynn J., Samantha J., Kristina S.,
Kalista B., Micci S., Brianna I., Patrona C., Kaitlyn L., Ally M.,
Keyra M., Sabrina C., Gracie B., Zoey R., Kristen S., Kaitlyn W.,
and you!*

—J. H. and S. W.

CONTENTS

1

Cheer

Pallas

SQUEE! PALLAS WAS BURSTING WITH EXCITEMENT.

She and the other two dozen mortal students on the

Triton Junior High cheer and swordplay team were in

a flying chariot, heading to perform at a shopping mall

called the Immortal Marketplace. The IM was located

halfway between Earth, where they lived, and Mount

Olympus, where godboys and goddessgirls lived.

Officially named the Cheer Blades, her team often marched with the school band and did feats such as sword-tossing, sword-wielding, and battle arts exhibitions at TJH athletic events. But it was a special honor to have been invited to do a choreographed routine for immortals at the IM today!

Pallas loved performing. And since it was Saturday morning, there would probably be lots of shoppers around to watch them. But there was also another reason she could hardly wait to get to the marketplace. She'd invited her BFF—the goddessgirl Athena—to come watch the show.

Would Athena come, though? She hadn't answered Pallas's invitation. Or the last five letterscrolls Pallas had sent before the invitation. Up until these last letterscrolls, Athena had been replying to any letters Pallas sent. But then for some reason Athena had begun ignoring her. Which kind of hurt her feelings.

In her letters Pallas had tried not to sound lonely and sad about how much she missed Athena, and she had tried not to put any pressure on her BFF to come to today's performance. Instead, Pallas had written in an upbeat tone about funny things that had happened at school and about how much fun she'd been having. But still no reply from Athena.

"Nice sword," a snarky voice suddenly piped up.

Startled, Pallas brushed away a windblown strand of her long, purple-streaked black hair to see that another team's chariot had moved closer and was flying alongside the Cheer Blades' chariot now. And a mortal girl passenger inside it was eyeing Pallas's sword critically. Farther off there were three other flying chariots as well, each containing mortal students from various Earth schools. All in all, five teams would be performing at the IM today.

Pallas's attention snapped over to the snarky girl's friend, who added, "Yeah, *reeeal* nice." The two unknown girls giggled. They were sitting together, craning their necks to view Pallas's sword.

Unsure what to reply, she scooted the sword behind her leg so that it was less visible. She knew they were just being mean because her sword was not at all nice. In fact, it was downright ugly. Made of iron (which was surprisingly soft unless mixed with stronger metals), it had tons of little dents and rusted patches along the blade. And it was tremendously old, too—as old as her dad!

It had been his sword when he was a boy, and he treasured it. He'd given it to her when she'd joined the cheer and swordplay team at Triton Junior High. She had taken it because . . . well, what choice did she have? She needed a sword to be on the team, plus she hadn't wanted to seem ungrateful or hurt his feelings.

Besides, their family didn't have the money to buy a flashy brand-new sword. Pallas had been baby-sitting for various neighbors in Triton lately, though, and had been saving her earnings from those jobs. It was fun taking care of little kids, but she was a long way from having saved enough drachmas to buy a new sword. So in the meantime she was stuck with this ugly, old-fashioned, embarrassing one.

As the two mean girls in the other chariot continued to stare, Pallas forced a bright smile. "Thanks!" she called over at last. "My goddessgirl friend Athena really admires my sword too."

Embarrassment had made her angry, and she'd meant to put the two girls in their place. However, the minute the words slipped out, she wished she could call them back.

Students in both chariots who'd heard her boast went quiet, perking up at the mention of the mega-famous goddessgirl Athena. That included the girl Pallas was sharing a seat with—her favorite mortal friend from TJH, Eurynome.

"You're friends with Athena?" asked the snarky girl from the other chariot. Only now she sounded awestruck instead of critical.

"Will she be at the IM today? Can you help us meet her? And get her autograph?" the snarky girl's friend asked eagerly.

"Maybe," Pallas replied, though she wasn't really sure about all that.

Eurynome leaned over Pallas. Striving to be heard over the whooshing wind, she shouted to them, "Maybe shmyabe. Of course she can. Pallas and Athena used to be BFFs!"

Still are, Pallas wanted to say. But something stopped her. A feeling of uncertainty. She and Athena had grown up together like sisters in the same house on the banks of the Triton River. They'd attended TJH together until Athena had been invited . . . *ordered*, really . . . to attend Mount Olympus Academy.

Would Athena show up at the IM for the performance today? Or was she trying to send Pallas a message by *not* replying to her invitation—a message that she didn't want to be friends anymore? Pallas's stomach tightened.

"Wow!" said the snarky girl from the other school. "So what about that autograph? Will you help us? C'mon, be a pal."

Pallas shrugged. She didn't want to be this mean girl's pal! No way.

Eurynome seemed to sense from Pallas's hesitation that something was wrong. She jumped into the conversation again, switching gears. Trying to give Pallas an out now, she told the two mean girls, "On the other hand, immortals are busy people. They don't have time for autographs, and Pallas might not want to push her friendship like that."

"Mm-hm." As Pallas nodded in agreement, the snarky girl's chariot veered away, out of talking range. Discussion over. *Phew!*

"Talk about pushy, huh?" Eurynome said to Pallas, rolling her eyes.

Pallas nodded, rolling her eyes too. Then they grinned at each other.

Eurynome had only started at TJH one month

before Athena had moved away. After Athena was gone Pallas and Eurynome had both tried out for and made the Cheer Blades team. That had led to hanging out and practicing sword drills together, like Pallas and Athena had done before Athena had left.

Pallas was a little worried Eurynome was starting to think they were becoming BFFs. Which wasn't the case. Eurynome was fun, but still, their friendship was *not* the same as Pallas's friendship with Athena.

Back when Athena had lived in Triton and gone to TJH, she and Pallas had laughed at all the same jokes and shared many of the same interests. They'd been so attuned to each other that they could even finish each other's sentences!

The truth was that Pallas couldn't commit to being BFFs with anyone from Triton. Because she already had a BFF—Athena! At least she hoped that was still true.

"Think Zeus will be at the IM today?" she heard a girl at the front of the chariot ask their coach.

"It's possible but unlikely," their coach replied. "There are many demands on his time. So as much as he might like to, he can't become involved in every event."

Humph! Sometimes when she was feeling especially lonely, Pallas almost wished Zeus had not found time to "get involved" in her and Athena's lives. Or at least in Athena's. Because of him, Athena hadn't been around to hang out with her ever since Doom Day. That was what Pallas had mentally nicknamed the fateful day earlier in the school year when a scroll from Zeus had suddenly dropped its newsbomb on them.

Turned out Zeus was Athena's dad! And his other

big news had been that she was a goddessgirl! Both things had come as a whopping surprise. Not only that, but he had commanded that she change schools and start at Mount Olympus Academy right away.

Zeus was also the King of the Gods, Ruler of the Heavens, and the principal of the Academy. Therefore, even though Athena had been unsure about going, she had obeyed his orders. The very next day a chariot much like the one the Cheer Blades rode in now, only smaller, had whisked her away to MOA. Athena had not been back to Triton since.

Pallas's thoughts were interrupted when a girl in her chariot abruptly burst into a cheer. It was one they sometimes did while seated in the stands at TJH athletic events. It was fun and involved clashing their swords and stomping their feet in a rhythmic pattern.

Between chanted verses, each pair of cheer partners would clank the flats of their swords' blades, making a noise that sounded almost like cymbals crashing together! The cheer went like this:

> *"We're the Cheer Blades and we say,*
>
> *Our team wants to win today!"*
>
> *Clank! Stomp!*
>
> *Clank! Stomp! Stomp!*
>
> *"And you know one thing is true,*
>
> *No one stomps the Triton crew!"*
>
> *Clank! Stomp!*
>
> *Clank! Stomp! Stomp!*
>
> *"'Cause when the Tritons rock the field,*
>
> *All the other teams must yield!"*
>
> *Clank! Stomp!*
>
> *Clank! Stomp! Stomp!*

After performing it now, the entire cheer team erupted in hoots and whoops.

When the excitement died down, a girl seated in front of Pallas turned around. "So you've been to Mount Olympus Academy, right?" she asked. "What's it like?"

Pallas acted all casual like she always did when asked this question. Ever since the single time when Athena had summoned her to spend the night at MOA, she had been questioned about the details of her visit so often that she had memorized her response by heart.

"It's, you know . . . majestic," she began, gesturing with her hands to indicate the splendidness of the Academy. "Polished white stone sparkling in the sunlight atop the highest mountain in Greece; tall Ionic pillars on all sides; five stories high; marble tiles on

13

the floors; paintings on the ceilings showing the glorious exploits of the gods and goddesses. Like that."

Eurynome nudged her with a slight shoulder bump. "Don't forget about the lunch lady."

Pallas nodded, feeling like an actor repeating lines. "Oh, yeah. The main cafeteria lady has eight arms," she added on cue.

"Did you get to taste any ambrosia or nectar?" another girl across the aisle asked her excitedly.

"Obviously not, or her skin would be glittery," replied the girl who'd asked about MOA.

A third TJH girl two rows ahead replied, "Hello? Did you fail Immortal Studies or something? Eating and drinking that stuff wouldn't make her skin look glittery. It only affects immortals that way. See? Like those goddessgirls." She leaned over the side of the chariot to point out a group of four immortals flying in the distance. Everyone, including Pallas, whipped around to look.

The four goddessgirls were whizzing along together on winged sandals, moving toward the IM from the opposite direction. Though they were still a ways off, Pallas recognized Athena immediately. A thrill shot through her, and she waved and called out, "Athena!"

Her BFF didn't respond. She must be too far away to hear, Pallas decided. Maybe when they drew closer, she could try to get Athena's attention again.

"Who are the other three? I can't see them very well," a girl seated behind Pallas wondered.

"The golden-haired one in pink is Aphrodite, the goddessgirl of love and beauty," said Pallas. "And see? There's Persephone, with the flowers in her long, red hair."

"And Artemis!" said Eurynome. "She's easy to spot, with that quiver of arrows slung across her back and carrying an archery bow."

The students from Triton Junior High got all excited. Acting starstruck, they rushed to the side of the chariot and waved and yelled greetings to the immortals. Hearing them at last, the four goddess-girls waved back. Everyone was making too much noise for Pallas to catch Athena's attention, though.

Suddenly their chariot tipped dangerously to one side. *Ye gods!* With everyone rushing across the aisle to wave from Pallas's side, the chariot had gotten unbalanced.

"Take your seats!" hollered their coach, who was driving. Quickly the mortal girls took their proper places, and the chariot righted itself. Their flying chariot was part of a fleet whose magic worked for mortals as well as immortals. Zeus had begun lending them out to encourage mortals to visit the IM more often to shop. Luckily, they hadn't wrecked it just now! But by the time Pallas located the four goddessgirls again, they were barely within sight, continuing on in the direction of the IM.

Sigh. She'd missed her chance. Still, she was excited to have spotted Athena. Her BFF must've taken Pallas up on her invitation to this event after all. She was coming to the performance. At long last they'd get to hang out like in the good old days.

Fifteen minutes later the Cheer Blades' chariot landed outside the IM along with the other four mortal teams' chariots. Pallas's team piled out. Directed by their coach, they marched with their swords at their sides, moving single file into the marketplace.

"Wow, there are tons of people here!" said

Eurynome, sounding excited and a little nervous.

"I guess Zeus's plan is working," said Pallas.

According to an article they'd read in the *Greekly Weekly News* recently, shoppers had been avoiding the IM after a blowhard monster named Typhon had terrorized Greece and then attacked Mount Olympus. To make mortals feel welcome at the IM again, Zeus had begun providing free chariot transportation from Earth. He had also been inviting in entertainment like the Cheer Blades to help boost traffic and bring in business for the shopkeepers.

Pallas moved her head this way and that, hoping to spot Athena again. There she was, standing across the atrium, in the crowd near a large central fountain.

Till now Pallas had been feeling kind of mad at Athena for not replying to any of her recent letter-scrolls. But upon seeing her again, memories of their friendship flooded back, and Pallas was dying to go over and say hi and hug her. Unfortunately, her coach wouldn't be happy if she broke formation or shouted out.

Pallas kept her eyes on Athena, willing her to look over. To her disappointment her BFF seemed oblivious to her presence. She and her goddessgirl friends were now talking to some boys. *Boys?* She and Athena hadn't been much interested in them back when Athena had lived in Triton.

The two of them had kind of been outsiders. Mostly because of what Athena had called her own "weirdness." Pallas hadn't minded, though. No matter what anyone else had thought, she'd known her BFF was mega-cool.

Because even back then Athena had been supersmart and exceptional in many ways. She had learned

19

to knit *and* do math when she was only three years old. And in elementary school she had invented the flute and the trumpet, and had played an impromptu concert, even though she'd known nothing about music.

And then there was the time when Athena's feet had left the ground and her hair had turned into bristly brown owl feathers. Right in the middle of gym class! Although she had changed back almost immediately, some kids had nicknamed her "Birdbrain" as a result. They'd stopped all their teasing when it had turned out that the "weirdness" was an indication that Athena was in fact a goddessgirl.

"Students, be seated!" At their coach's signal, Pallas and the rest of her team took their assigned seats in chairs that had been set up around a temporary elevated stage in the wide aisle between the shops. Along with the other teams, they awaited their turn to perform. The Cheer Blades were scheduled last, so they watched the other groups do their routines first. Pallas kept turning her head, trying to catch Athena's eye, but Athena was still off in the thick of the audience and too far away to notice her.

Since the Cheer Blades were wearing their newly redesigned purple uniforms trimmed in white, Pallas realized Athena might not recognize them as being from TJH. Plus, Pallas's dark, wavy hair looked different with the matching purple streaks she'd added especially for this occasion. Surely once they got onstage, Athena would recognize her, though.

As the third team performed, Pallas bounced in her seat, feeling a bit antsy to get onstage. Would Athena be impressed by the skills Pallas had acquired since they had last practiced together? To be sure, her dad's banged-up old sword wasn't very impressive, but Athena wasn't stuck-up. She'd seen that sword many times back when she and Pallas had shared a bedroom in Triton. And she'd never once made fun of it.

Finally it was the TJH team's turn. They marched onstage and lined up in formation. As one of the best members of the team, Pallas took her place front and center. Athena couldn't miss her now!

The music began, and the Cheer Blades unsheathed and brandished their swords in a carefully orchestrated routine they'd practiced a gazillion times. Pallas put out her best effort, kind of showing off a little.

During a pause in the routine, Pallas scanned the crowd. Where was Athena? She wasn't standing where she'd been before. Had she moved, or . . . left?

Her attention diverted, Pallas was a few seconds

late with the next move. Trying to catch up, she swung her sword a bit too hard. *Clank!*

Its iron blade hit her teammate's newer, stronger steel blade in the wrong way. With a sad creak, the sword Pallas held twisted in the middle and bent sideways.

Oh no! It was now impossibly mangled—right in the middle of the most important routine her team had ever performed!

2

Lettuce

Athena

I T WAS SATURDAY, MIDMORNING, AND ATHENA and her three GGBFFs (Goddessgirl Best Friends Forever)—Aphrodite, Artemis, and Persephone—had just landed at the Immortal Marketplace. Athena had come to shop for a sword at Mighty Fighty—a store that also sold spears, javelins, bows and arrows, shields, armor, and athletic stuff. Because in one week there was going to be a spectacular swordplay competition at the Greek Fest, a festival she had been put in charge of down on Earth.

Back when she'd lived in Triton, she and her old friend Pallas had practiced their swordplay skills almost every day after school. But since enrolling at Mount Olympus Academy, Athena had gotten really busy, and her sword skills had grown rusty.

Luckily, her dad, Zeus, had offered to spar with her tomorrow on the MOA sports fields to help bring her back up to speed. She would use the new sword she bought not only for their practice but also in the swordplay competition.

"Ready for some sword shopping?" Artemis asked her eagerly. Since Artemis excelled at archery—and most other sports too—she had promised to help Athena pick out a sword.

"Sure," said Athena.

Aphrodite had come with them because she wanted to buy makeup. Persephone was here too and was the first of them to dash away after they'd entered the IM. "I'm off to help out at my mom's shop. Have fun, you guys!" she called to them over her shoulder. Her mom owned Demeter's Daisies, Daffodils, and Floral Delights, a flower shop in the marketplace.

As Athena, Aphrodite, and Artemis passed the Oracle-O Bakery and Scrollbooks shop on the way to the atrium, they waved through the shop window to a girl with fire-gold hair named Cassandra. Her family owned the shop, and she was busy helping customers inside.

Just then two mortal boys came out of the bakery munching cookies they'd bought. Though not on purpose, the goddessgirls wound up trailing them. They were passing a fancy carousel with fantastical animal rides that the immortals had helped build earlier that year, when Artemis pointed one of the boys out. "Hey, who's that guy up ahead? He looks familiar."

"The tough-looking one with the red hair? That's Agamemnon. He's that mortal who was crushing on Cassandra, until Apollo stole her affections," explained Aphrodite. As the goddessgirl of love and beauty, she could be depended on to know who was crushing on who at any given moment.

"What?" a boy's voice huffed from behind them. "I never knew about that!" Athena and her friends turned to see Artemis's twin brother, Apollo, on their heels. So was one of his best godboy buds, Ares, who was Aphrodite's crush.

"Oops," said Aphrodite, her pretty blue eyes going wide. "Forget I said anything."

Walking backward now, Artemis spoke to her brother. "Calm down. You have nothing to worry about. That Agamemnon is a bully, and I heard that Cassandra never liked him." Artemis and Apollo were twins, but she was a few minutes older. Because of that, she often felt it her duty to advise or soothe him when he was upset.

However, today her words only seemed to make matters worse. Concluding that Agamemnon must have bullied his crush as well as crushed on her, Apollo eyed the mortal boy's back fiercely.

"That guy with him is Achilles," said Ares, glaring at the boys in front of them too. Achilles had glossy black hair that was short on the sides and longish on top. "He's okay. Except that he hangs out with that loser Agamemnon. I think they both go to the same school."

"Yeah, same school as Cassandra," said Apollo. His scowl deepened. Apollo and Ares started to move toward the boys, but were unexpectedly blocked by a gathering crowd.

"What's going on?" wondered Artemis, looking around in surprise.

It was hard to see over the heads of all the people and the large fountain at the atrium's center. However, when Athena stood on tiptoe, she managed to spot a bunch of mortal girls marching up to stand on a stage in the wide main aisle that ran between the IM shops. The girls were holding swords and lining up in cheer team formation.

"Mega-cool!" Athena said. "Looks like there's going to be a swordplay performance. My dad must've thought this up. He's been doing a great job of booking entertainment to bring more shoppers to the IM, don't you think? Did you guys come to watch this exhibition?" She knew she was jabbering, but she was trying to change the subject in hopes of calming Apollo and Ares down. It worked, sort of.

Music began, and the two godboys looked toward the stage with interest. But as the first team began their performance, Apollo and Ares' faces reflected disappointment.

"Argh! We came because we heard there would be swordplay. But we didn't know it was going to be all girls," Ares said glumly.

"Girls doing *cheers*," added Apollo, sighing.

Aphrodite lifted an eyebrow. "Is that a problem?" She, Athena, Persephone, and Artemis were all on the MOA Cheer team.

Artemis folded her arms, frowning at the boys. "Cheer is a very physically demanding sport, you know."

"And as you also know, lots of girls rock at sword-play," Athena informed them.

Seeming to sense that they were losing this battle of words, Ares held up his hands, palms outward. "Okay, okay, let's not fight about it," he said. Which made everyone laugh, because he was the godboy of war and usually adored fighting—the physical kind, anyway!

While they all continued to watch the performance, Athena suddenly realized two things. One, Agamemnon and Achilles had disappeared from view. And two, the mortals who had waved at her and her friends from their chariot were probably among the teams here. She wished she could see the insignia on their school uniforms, but distance and the crowds surrounding the stage made that impossible.

"This is fun," she said after a few more minutes

passed. "But I've got to get going to Mighty Fighty."
She turned to leave, and Aphrodite and Artemis
did too.

"Mighty Fighty?" Ares echoed. Instantly his and
Apollo's expressions brightened and they started
tagging along.

"I'm meeting my dad tomorrow to spar in prepa-
ration for the Greek Fest, so I need a new sword,"
Athena explained as the group walked along. "After
I snag one, I'll have to hurry back to the MOA dorm.
Hero-ology and Science-ology homework awaits."

"Overachiever," Aphrodite teased her.

Athena grinned. In addition to being on the Cheer
Squad, she was also the goddessgirl of inventing,
battle, weaving, and wisdom, among other things.
She just had so many interests! Her MOA friends all
knew she enjoyed taking tons of classes and stuffed

as many extracurriculars into her schedule as possible.

"We'll come help you choose a sword," Ares offered, and Apollo nodded eagerly.

Artemis rolled her eyes. "Athena's the goddessgirl of battle. I think she can handle the decision on her own. With a little help from me, of course."

Athena laughed. "I only *inspire* heroes to excel in battle, though. Ares is really the expert when it comes to weaponry and actual fighting. I'd be glad to hear advice from all of you. I'm hoping that if I put in a glorious appearance in full battle gear at the Greek Fest, it will inspire everyone else there to do their best in the competitions!"

The festival was to be held in Athens, a city in Greece that had been named for her after she had beat the godboy of the sea, Poseidon, in an invention contest. Her winning invention had been the small, seemingly unimportant olive. Turned out that Greek mortals had found many uses for the small fruit, including as fuel oil, food, and olive wood for building homes.

"I'll stop in here," said Aphrodite as the group passed a shop called Cleo's Cosmetics. "I need supplies for a Beauty-ology project. My class is going to offer youthful makeovers for any MOA teachers who dare to volunteer." With a farewell wave and a "Catch you later," she went into the shop.

Not long afterward, Athena and Artemis stood in Mighty Fighty, the only girl customers among a whole bunch of mortal and immortal boys. The bunch included the red-haired Agamemnon and his dark-haired friend Achilles, unfortunately. Those boys were *ooh*ing and *aah*ing over something in the sword department.

Avoiding that department for the moment, Athena

led Apollo and Ares to the other side of the store, claiming fascination with a spear display there. When she glanced back, Agamemnon was holding a sword high and eyeing along its blade as if to make sure it was straight. "What do you think of this one?" he asked Achilles. His voice was loud enough to be heard throughout the store.

"Looks good." Achilles reached for a different sword, but Agamemnon quickly grabbed it first, discarding the sword he'd originally chosen. "Sorry, bud. Changed my mind."

Achilles just shrugged and sorted through some others. "It's okay. I didn't really want that one, anyway. I'm looking for the perfect sword. One I can name Briseis."

"'Briseis'?" Agamemnon scoffed. "You're going to name your sword?"

"Sure, why not?" said Achilles, picking up a new sword. "It'll be cool."

Agamemnon smirked. "Uh-huh. I bet it's the name of some girl you're crushing on, right?" he teased. Athena noticed that Agamemnon was now jealously eyeing the new sword that Achilles had picked up.

"No, but if we're naming swords after crushes, maybe you should name the one you buy Cassandra," Achilles teased back.

Hearing this, Apollo frowned at the mortal boys and nudged Ares, nodding toward them.

"That's over," said Agamemnon. He and Achilles seemed unaware that Apollo and Ares were watching them. "Maybe I'll call whatever sword I buy Evgenís instead."

"A noble name," joked Achilles. Because "noble" was what the word "Evgenís" meant!

Agamemnon sent him a mischievous glance. "Think Cassandra will like it?"

Achilles laughed. "Thought you were over her."

Agamemnon just grinned. From the corner of her eye, Athena saw him sneakily glance across the store at Apollo and Ares. That meanie! Apparently he'd known for a while that the godboys were there, and was just trying to stir up trouble!

Artemis stepped in front of Ares and her brother when they began to move toward the other boys. "Ignore them," she advised Apollo. "He knows Cassandra likes you, so he's only aiming to pick a fight."

"She's right. Agamemnon seems the type who always wants what others have," Athena added quietly.

Sure enough, the next time Achilles picked up a sword, Agamemnon pushed to trade again. Achilles reluctantly agreed, probably to avoid an argument.

But then Agamemnon seemed to lose interest in the new sword, like he feared he'd made a bad trade.

"What a creep," Artemis murmured.

Needing to get moving on her *own* selection, Athena edged closer to the sword department. Apollo and Ares followed.

After picking up two swords, one in each hand, she tested their weight and inspected their blades for straightness. Then she looked from one godboy to the other, hoping to keep their attention off fighting with the mortals. "Ares? Apollo? Can you help me choose between these?"

Her plan backfired because Agamemnon over-heard. Pointedly ignoring Apollo, he eagerly sought out the godboy of war's opinion on the swords he and his friend now held. "Hey, Ares? Which sword do you think is better? Mine or Achilles'?"

Before Ares could respond, Apollo butted in. "Excellence is more about the talent of the swordsman than the sword. Which tells me you're in trouble no matter what sword you choose," he told Agamemnon rudely.

"What's that supposed to mean?" Agamemnon demanded, his chin jutting out.

Apollo's meaning had seemed pretty clear to Athena. Was Agamemnon a little dimwitted, maybe? He was begging for a fight, whether he knew it or not.

"I think I'll take this sword," Athena said, desperately trying to draw the godboys' attention. "Ares? Apollo? Any thoughts?" Seeing that they were in no mood to weigh in with their opinions, Athena headed for the checkout counter to make her purchase anyway.

Artemis was still doing her best to calm Apollo

down when Athena returned to them with the sword in a shopping bag. Fortunately, before the godboys and mortal boys could come to blows, something astonishing happened. Out in the main aisle of the marketplace, people began running past the store's window, hooting and shouting.

Suddenly Aphrodite burst into Mighty Fighty, holding a shopping bag bearing the Cleo's Cosmetics logo. "Athena! Thank godness! Come quick. It's Hera!"

"What's wrong?" asked Athena, fearing that something awful must've happened to her stepmother.

"Not sure exactly. I just heard she's at the Hungry, Hungry Harpy Café and that something weird is going on with her. Something weird enough to attract a crowd. C'mon!"

"Go!" urged Artemis, shooing them out of the

shop along with Ares and Apollo. Then she stayed behind, blocking the door to make sure Agamemnon and Achilles couldn't follow.

Seconds later Athena was grabbing a pair of H-shaped door handles and pushing into the café. It seemed half the IM was already there, drawn by the excitement. Among the shopkeepers and customers in the café, she spotted Cleo, the three-eyed owner of Cleo's Cosmetics, and Mr. Dolos, whose shop sold hero mementos.

"Keep an eye on your stuff," Athena heard someone caution as she made her way through the crowd. Automatically she clasped her shopping bag extra tightly. The Harpies that owned this café were known pickpockets. If you didn't watch your plate, they'd steal the food they'd served you right off it!

Although they had pretty faces and normal hair,

the sisters were covered with bird feathers, had bird-claw feet, and liked to fly on scavenger hunts. A collection of oddities they'd snatched from far and wide was proudly displayed right here on the café's walls, shelves, and ceiling—including a baby bottle they claimed had once belonged to a baby Zeus.

Worried, Athena hurriedly nudged her way through the onlookers, leaving Aphrodite, Apollo, and Ares somewhere behind in the crowd. She came to a halt a half dozen feet from her stepmom. Hera was sitting in a dining booth, looking surprisingly unharmed.

"Are you okay? What's going on?" Athena asked her in confusion.

"I'm fine. Better than fine!" said Hera, rising to her feet. There was a joyful light in her face, and she was smiling. "Look!" She gestured toward a three-tiered stone fountain that stood nearby. It was about as tall as Hera was, and the water in its bottom two tiers was bubbling merrily. Its top tier held a big green ball, Athena noticed, but no water.

"Nice. A new artifact the Harpies acquired, I presume?" asked Athena, totally bewildered. All this fuss was about some old stone fountain?

As Athena watched, Hera reached with both arms toward the top of the fountain. The green ball was actually made of crisp green leaves, Athena saw now. As Hera's hands touched it, the leaves magically peeled back and opened, as if hinged. It was like a beach-ball-sized oyster made out of lettuce leaves!

A gasp of delight rippled over the crowd. Because this leafy oyster didn't contain a pearl. Instead, it held . . . *a real live baby girl*! Athena could tell it was a girl because a golden wreath embossed with the words "It's a girl!" crowned the baby's wispy brown hair.

Hera gently lifted the infant from the lettuce leaves to cradle it in her arms.

Athena smiled, relieved that her stepmom didn't appear injured after all. "What's a baby doing in a fountain?" Athena murmured, but no reply came. This baby couldn't be a Naiad, could she? No, those were freshwater-swimming, mermaid-like nymphs that lived in rivers and fountains. And this tiny girl didn't have a mermaid tail. Her cute little arms and legs were wriggling.

Stepping closer, Athena smiled at the baby, and it gurgle-smiled back.

Hera owned a wedding shop in the IM. So did this baby belong to one of the brides she'd helped get married sometime back? Athena looked around, wondering which woman here might be the baby's mom.

The crowd began to applaud and *ooh* and *aah* over the baby. Several of Hera's shop assistants, who were also in the café, startled Athena by coming over and hugging her. "Congratulations!" they said merrily.

Athena smiled at them. "For what?" She often won awards and contests, but she hadn't won any new ones lately.

"On the baby, of course!" a woman standing across from her said.

"Huh? Whose is it?" replied Athena.

Whereupon Hera smiled broadly and beckoned her even closer. "Athena! Isn't it wonderful? You're a big sister!"

"What?" Athena's jaw dropped. Slowly it dawned on her. This baby was *Hera's* baby! That meant it was Athena's half sister, since Hera was married to her dad.

Aphrodite finally made her way through the crowd to Athena's side and gave her a hug. "You are sooo lucky! I've always wished I had a little sister. She's adorable!"

Others came over and hugged Athena too, but she just stood there, stunned. She tried hard to wrap her brain around the idea that this baby was now part of her family. However, although her brain usually worked very well, it wasn't quite grasping that she actually had a baby sister. Maybe because her brain didn't really want to.

Finally she found her voice. "But . . . I just saw Dad yesterday. He didn't say anything about a baby," she protested. Was this baby adopted? Had her parents really made such a huge family decision without telling her? It seemed so.

Since Hera wasn't Athena's *real* mom, was that why

Hera hadn't thought she needed to include Athena in this decision? Athena's real mom was a fly named Metis. But one day she had flown off forever to be with her fly buddies. After that, Zeus and Hera had met at an MOA school dance and then, later, had married. Athena had grown to love Hera, so it hurt to have a surprise baby sister sprung on her like this.

Artemis had arrived in the café at some point and now pushed her way to Athena's side, with Apollo in tow. "Tell Athena what you just told me," she instructed her brother.

"Okay, okay." Apollo pointed to one of the café tables. "So earlier today, before Ares and I saw you girls in the atrium, we were eating breakfast over there. And then Hera came in, sat at the next table, and ordered a lettuce wrap scramble."

"I've had those," Artemis put in. "Scrambled eggs

47

and other stuff piled on a kind of lettuce called Hebe. Yummy."

"Yeah, so anyway," Apollo continued, "after Hera got her order, out of nowhere she says something like, 'I think Zeus and I are going to have a baby.' Next thing you know, that fountain over there appeared like magic."

He shuffled his feet and sent Athena an apologetic look. "I guess I should have said something to warn you, but I honestly wasn't sure what was going on. Ares and I left before the baby appeared—er, was born in the fountain."

"This is crazy," said Athena, shaking her head. Hera had proved to be an awesome stepmom, kind and patient and full of good advice. Now in an instant, Athena felt like she had lost her, or part of her anyway, to a leafy bundle of baby.

"Well, it's not the weirdest immortal birth ever," Aphrodite reminded her. "You sprang right out of Zeus's head. And I was born out of sea foam." Aphrodite sounded pretty cool about this now, but when Athena had first come to MOA, it had been a touchy subject. Mostly because Medusa, a snake-haired MOA student, used to tease Aphrodite about it.

"Also, I'm not sure if I ever told you this," Artemis put in, "but right after Apollo and I were born, I started helping my mom take care of him." This was a story Athena had never heard before. And from the look on Aphrodite's face, she'd never heard it either.

"And Aphrodite called *me* the overachiever? I think maybe you deserve that title instead," Athena teased Artemis. Which made them all giggle.

WHAM! Athena and most of the crowd jumped as the café doors were abruptly shoved wide open. Zeus burst in, bright sparks of electricity crackling up and down his great muscled arms. This usually happened when he was either super-mad or super-happy. The sparkle in his blue eyes and his wide smile showed how he felt now.

"Just heard the big news!" he announced in his booming voice. "Is it true? I'm a dad again?"

"Yes! Our newborn daughter magically appeared in a lettuce wrap!" Hera called out as she beckoned him over.

The crowd parted, and Zeus rushed to her side. He leaned over her to gaze at the tiny bundle of baby in her arms as Hera explained more of what had happened. When he held out a finger and the baby grabbed it in her little fist, Zeus's face lit with joy. "She's magnificent! And she's got my grip! Let's name her Hebe after the lettuce she was born in."

Hera smiled happily. "The perfect name for our perfect baby," she told Zeus. They looked very proud holding their new child.

Athena tried to act happy too, but her emotions were a mixed-up mess. Sure the baby was cute, and it might be fun to be a big sister. However, she was used to being Zeus's favorite and *one and only* daughter. It felt weird to be shoved aside as everyone focused on the new baby.

Suddenly, artists and reporters rushed into the café to make drawings and get the full scoop on the new baby, and Athena found herself shoved aside *literally*. By the next day their stories and drawings would likely appear in special issues of *Teen Scrollazine* and *Greekly Weekly News*. Within days the whole world would know about this surprise baby.

Athena slowly eased away from the center of things,

backing out through the crowd. No one noticed, not even her friends. All the focus was on Hebe. When Athena finally reached the door, she quietly opened it and slipped out into the atrium.

It was for the best that no one noticed her leave-taking, because she just couldn't pretend to be thrilled right now, and the last thing she wanted to do was spoil anyone else's pleasure in Hera's big news.

But what was she supposed to do with the unhappy feelings that were bubbling up inside her? She'd be too embarrassed to admit them out loud. Because the truth was, she was a teeny bit jealous. Maybe even more than a teeny bit. She couldn't tell her BFFs. She'd look like a big meanie or a big baby herself if she said she was jealous of her own baby sister.

Jealousy was not a proper emotion for a goddessgirl to feel, in her opinion. Still, she just couldn't help it!

As she zoomed home alone in her winged sandals, a couple of tears trickled down her cheeks before being swept away by the wind. They weren't happy tears either. She had a feeling that things were about to change big-time for her. If she'd had a few months—even a few *days*—to get used to the idea of a baby sister, maybe she would have felt differently. But this was just so sudden!

Well, tomorrow she would be meeting Zeus for their swordplay practice. The thought cheered her up. Hopefully their time together would calm her and make her feel more secure about her place in things. Feeling at least somewhat comforted, she touched down in the MOA courtyard.

3

Swords

Pallas

After her sword broke onstage in the IM cheer performance, Pallas froze for a few seconds. Then her many hours of Cheer Blades training kicked in. She continued to go through the motions, holding her sword's grip and pretending its blade was still straight and true, instead of partly bent and twisted in the middle. The rest of the routine seemed to last ten times longer than normal. But finally it ended and she and her team filed offstage.

The mangled, ridiculous-looking sword bumped her leg with every step, causing her heart to sink lower and lower. This disaster had been all her fault. She'd gotten distracted, looking around for Athena instead of paying strict attention to her routine. Because she'd gotten sloppy, her dad's sword was now totally messed up.

Even if she hadn't thought his sword was all that great, her dad treasured it. Her stomach tightened at the thought of how upset he was going to be when he saw it. Not that he'd blame her for what had happened. He was too nice to do that. But she would still blame herself. Too bad her dad didn't have a goddessgirl like Athena for a daughter. Because Athena probably never disappointed Zeus!

As Pallas and the rest of the Cheer Blades filed past another team, Pallas heard someone in the seats snicker. It was that snarky girl who'd spoken to her on the way over.

"Oh, be quiet," Pallas grumbled. She wasn't sure if the girl heard her or not, but her grumbling just made her feel worse, because she knew it was bad sportsmanship.

After they were seated, she felt Eurynome's eyes on her. "It's okay. We'll fix your sword or get you another one," her friend said kindly.

Pallas nodded, though she doubted either was possible. As final announcements were made, her eyes scanned the crowd. Athena had definitely disappeared, without bothering to watch Pallas's team finish. Or even to say hi!

Uh-oh! The coach was coming over, and she looked

displeased. Pallas slumped in her seat a little, figuring she was about to get a talking-to. A well-deserved one, given her lack of focus during the performance.

However, the coach must've seen how upset she was, because she only patted Pallas's shoulder sympathetically. "You can use one of the extra swords in my office cabinet back at school for the next practice," she told Pallas.

"Thanks, Coach," Pallas murmured. It was a nice gesture. Nevertheless, her spirits took a nosedive. Those swords were super-banged-up, even uglier than her dad's sword. They were the kind used by newbies for swordplay practice.

Pallas was far from being a newbie. She was ranked number one on her team. There were some teammates who thought that growing up with Athena had given her a kind of magical advantage.

But that just wasn't true. Any advantage had come from *practice*, not magic. She and Athena had done a lot of sparring together once upon a time, but they'd been pretty equal in skill, despite the fact that Pallas wasn't immortal.

After her flop onstage, Pallas hoped Athena didn't think her skill had faded. Had Athena seen and been embarrassed for her? Was that why her BFF had left the performance early? If Pallas could find her in the marketplace, maybe she could talk to her and explain.

By now it was nearly noon, and a tasty buffet lunch for the teams had been set out on a long table in the atrium. After they'd eaten, all the students were allowed to leave their swords with their coaches and go look around the IM on their own.

"Everyone meet back at the chariots in two hours

for the trip home," one of the coaches announced. "Don't be late!"

Once they were released, some students immediately made a dash for the fantastical carousel near the atrium. Each of them called out to claim their favorite of the painted animal rides that the immortals had created.

"Dibs on Dionysus's leopard!"

"I want the swan one that Aphrodite made!"

"Hey! Let's go to that Mighty Fighty store we read about in *Teen Scrollazine*," Eurynome suggested to Pallas as they set off to explore.

Pallas grinned, her spirits lifting. "Sounds fun. We can drool over swords and other stuff we can't afford to buy," she said in a lighthearted tone.

Like most of the other students, she'd brought money to spend at the IM, though her few coins didn't amount to much. Certainly not enough to buy a replacement for her dad's sword. So far she'd only saved forty-two obeloi from her babysitting jobs, which equaled seven drachmas. A really good sword could cost a hundred drachmas.

Still, it would be fun to visit the store they'd heard so much about. While window-shopping along the way there, Pallas kept an eye out for Athena but didn't spot her. However, when they approached the store, Pallas saw Persephone, Aphrodite, and Artemis going in. Athena wasn't with them. Could she be inside Mighty Fighty already?

Hoping so, Pallas sped up, and Eurynome kept pace beside her. As they entered Mighty Fighty, Pallas overheard Aphrodite speak to a mortal boy with glossy black hair. "Achilles? Have you seen Athena?" the goddessgirl asked. "We were in the café a minute

60

ago, but she disappeared. We thought she might have come back here." While Eurynome went over to gaze at a display of expensive swords they definitely could not afford, Pallas ducked behind a shelf of spears to listen for Achilles' reply.

When he didn't say anything right away, Aphrodite went on. "You remember her, right? *That* girl." She pointed at a poster hanging on the wall of the store that was too far away for Pallas to see clearly.

Achilles nodded. "Sure, I remember. Everybody knows who Athena is. But—"

Now a red-haired mortal boy who'd been standing next to him butted into the conversation. "But she hasn't been back since she was in here before with you."

"Guess our BFF is MIA," Aphrodite said to her friends. "As in 'missing in action.'"

BFF? Pallas's heart felt like it had been jabbed

61

with one of the spears from the display next to her. She had known from her one and only visit to the Academy that Athena and these immortal girls had quickly become good friends. But *BFFs*?

Her gaze went to the golden necklaces the three goddessgirls wore. In *Teen Scrollazine* drawings, Pallas had seen Athena wearing an identical one. Now she wondered if the double-G charms dangling from their necklaces were a symbol of a BFF club.

"No archery practice with Apollo today?" Pallas heard the red-haired boy ask Artemis on her way out. After learning that Athena was not in the store, Artemis and the others had turned to go.

"Not that it's any of your beeswax, Agamemnon, but nope," Artemis said curtly. She gestured toward the poster Aphrodite had pointed out earlier. "He's busy all week practicing for the festival with some of his friends."

Once the goddessgirls were gone, Pallas made a beeline over to examine the poster. It was an advertisement for a celebration called Greek Fest, which was to be held at one of Athena's temples the next Saturday. Since Athena's picture was on the poster, maybe she was in charge of it?

According to the poster, there would be athletic games, game booths, and art events at the festival. And reenactment competitions in which pairs of swordfighters would re-create famous historic battles to entertain the audience!

"Wow! How fun is that!" she murmured to herself. The poster said there would be prizes (mostly battle equipment) for the winners of these competitions.

"I think I'll take this one after all," she overheard one of the mortal boys announce. She looked over to see the one named Achilles holding a sword and smoothing his fingers along the flat of its blade.

The boys had moved over to a sword display against the wall now, near where Eurynome was still examining swords that Pallas could never afford in a gazillion years. The red-haired Agamemnon quickly set the sword he had been looking at back on the shelf and gazed jealously at the one Achilles had chosen. "But that's the one I had my eye on before!" Agamemnon complained.

Achilles laughed easily. "Too late! You had your chance. This one's mine. Yes, this will be my Briseis."

"Aw, c'mon," the other boy whined. "You know I wanted it."

Achilles hesitated, looking reluctant. Then, with a huge sigh, he handed the sword over. "Okay, but I hope you're not thinking about using it in that festival contest. I'm sure you'd like to see Apollo humbled in a swordfight, but we're on suspension from sword-play competition through that weekend, remember?"

"We'll see," Agamemnon said cockily. "There's more than one way to beat an immortal." He took the sword that Achilles had called Briseis over to the counter to pay for it. Pallas noticed that Achilles gazed longingly after the sword. So if he had a claim on it, why had he parted with it and caved to his friend's wishes? After quickly choosing another sword for himself, Achilles went to buy it.

Just then Eurynome came to stand by Pallas. She must have heard the boys talking, or seen Pallas studying the poster, because now she looked it over too. "Hey! Battle reenactments. We should enter. That poster says one of the prizes is this fabulous sword. Perfect! I mean, it's exactly what you need."

Pallas gazed at the drawing of the prize sword.

Its strong-looking blade was shiny and carved with fanciful designs. There was even a small ruby jewel embedded in its handle! "Yeah, only I'd need a new sword to win that sword. I mean, I can't compete in a battle reenactment without one."

"I'll lend you mine," offered Eurynome.

"Thanks, but you'll need yours for Cheer Blades practice," Pallas replied, shaking her head. "And anyway, even though we're both good, immortals will be in the competition. Only a great, new-style sword would give us a fighting chance. Plus, that poster says there's an entry fee to compete. I can't pay it."

"C'mon. Stop being so negative." Eurynome put a hand on her hip. "Now pretend I'm you and repeat after me," she said in a strong voice. "I am the *best* swordsgirl on the Cheer Blades team. Why, I've even won bouts against the goddessgirl Athena. So I'm going to enter this contest and give it my best shot, because I believe I can win!" She punched a fist in the air in emphasis.

"Hey, did I hear you guys say you've fought Athena?"

Eurynome and Pallas jumped in surprise. Turning their heads, they saw Agamemnon approaching them with his new sword. Achilles was right behind him.

"*Sparred* with her," Pallas corrected.

"So do you live around here?" Agamemnon asked.

Eurynome shrugged. "Nuh-uh. We go to Triton Junior High."

"We're here with one of the sword exhibition teams that performed earlier," explained Pallas.

"Oh, yeah, we watched those. Nice work," said Achilles, smiling at her.

It was obvious he didn't recognize her as the

performer who'd messed up so badly onstage. Otherwise he wouldn't have been at all impressed, thought Pallas.

The red-haired boy introduced himself as Agamemnon. Then he gestured to his black-haired friend. "And he's Achilles." Which Pallas already knew from her eavesdropping, of course. Eurynome politely supplied their names in return.

Agamemnon jerked his chin toward the poster. "So you want to enter that competition? We'll pay your entry fee," he told them. At this offer, Achilles looked as startled as Pallas felt.

"Why would you do that?" she asked. The offer was too good to be true.

"Because those dumb immortals always think they can win everything, that's why. We'd like to see some mortals beat them this time," Agamemnon replied smoothly. "We'll train you both and lend you our new blades to enter the swordplay competition."

"What's the catch?" asked Eurynome.

"Simple. If you do win the grand prize sword, you'll turn it over to us," said Agamemnon.

"What?" scoffed Pallas. She noticed that he was doing most of the talking, and she had a feeling this was all his idea.

"He means that if you win, you'll give us the prize sword *in trade* for one of these new swords we just bought. Right, Ag?" Achilles put in.

Agamemnon looked at him in irritation. "Thanks a lot for the lame idea, Dip. But I guess we could do that, yeah."

Pallas scrunched her nose, wondering why he was calling Achilles "Dip." "Why should we be your champions? If we want to enter, we'll do it on our own."

"Yeah, we're already experts with swords," boasted Eurynome.

"Thought you said you didn't have the entry fee. And have you had the hours of training we've had at our school? Two hours after school every day, with competitions every weekend since kindergarten?" asked Agamemnon.

"Well, no. But if you've got so much training, why aren't you competing yourselves?" asked Eurynome. She fixed her gaze on Achilles as if wanting a reply from him instead of from Agamemnon this time.

"Uh." Achilles looked a little sheepish. His mouth opened and shut, but no explanation came forth.

Quickly Agamemnon jumped in to answer. "There's a reason, but we're sworn to secrecy."

Achilles shot him a surprised glance. Pallas had already overheard him say they'd been temporarily

70

suspended from swordplay competition. She guessed Agamemnon was embarrassed about that, and so he was trying to act cool and mysterious about why they wouldn't compete.

"Give us a sec," Eurynome told the boys. Then she pulled Pallas a short distance away to where they wouldn't be overheard.

"I just thought of something," Eurynome began. "Yesterday I was doing some homework on that Greek poet guy Hesiod. In his writings he said stuff about how the godboy Hephaestus has this amazing blacksmithing forge at Mount Olympus Academy. One time Hephaestus used it to make a shield for Dionysus that had constellations and cool things carved on it in silver and gold." She looked at Pallas expectantly, her brown eyes twinkling.

"So?" Pallas prompted, not understanding her point.

"So . . . if we did enter the Greek Fest thing, you could borrow one of those boys' swords to compete. But you could also bring your dad's sword. Then, if Hephaestus is at the festival, you could give it to him and ask him to fix it when he has time. He's got that great forge and all, so maybe he will. Especially if you tell him you're Athena's friend."

Pallas's mind began spinning with possibilities. Although both girls were already good with a sword, their actual training time was limited to one hour a day in Cheer Blades class. And part of that time was devoted to learning cheers and marches, not learning fight moves. So the boys' coaching actually could prove useful.

Besides that, if Athena *had* seen Pallas's snafu during the event in the atrium, performing well in the festival would prove Pallas hadn't turned into a klutz. She could redeem herself!

"So what do you think?" Eurynome nudged. "Remember, there's also the possibility we'd wind up with one of those boys' swords too."

"I'm in if you are," said Pallas. Eurynome grinned, and they high-fived.

After making a deal and a plan to train with Achilles and Agamemnon tomorrow and every day after school for the coming week, the girls left Mighty Fighty to head for the TJH chariot. Realistically, it was a longshot that she'd wind up with a new sword after the festival, Pallas knew. And if Hephaestus didn't agree to fix her dad's sword, there was no way she'd be able to afford to buy her dad a new one anytime soon. It would take a whole year of babysitting to buy just *half* a sword! Still, even a longshot was better than *no* shot.

On the chariot ride home, Eurynome said to Pallas,

"I meant what I said before. You are the best on the whole Cheer Blades team, better even than anyone on those other teams today too. I really do think you have a good chance to win that competition."

"Thanks. You do too, though," Pallas said encouragingly.

Just then someone in the chariot started a cheer, and the two girls happily joined in. No matter what happened, thought Pallas, at least she and Eurynome would get some additional training. And although they'd have to give up the grand prize if their longshot came through and one of them won next Saturday, they'd still wind up with one brand-spanking-new sword from those boys!

4

Baby

Athena

SUNDAY MORNING ATHENA WAS UP AND OUT ON
the MOA sports field an hour early for her swordplay practice with Zeus. She began by doing some
warm-up moves on her own to stretch out so that she
would be at her best when her dad arrived to spar
with her and give her pointers.

Artemis stopped by on a walk with her three

dogs, and the two goddessgirls discussed strategy and worked on some of Athena's stances. However, eventually Artemis ambled off with the hounds, leaving Athena to wait on the sports field. And wait and wait and wait. When Zeus was forty-five minutes late, she finally headed into the Academy to check on him and see if anything was wrong.

The minute she stepped into the main office, she saw Hebe's fountain from the café. It was hard to miss, since it sat in the middle of the office now. Curious to see how it worked, Athena walked around it. Weirdly, she could discover no source for the clear fresh water that still bubbled merrily in the lower two tiers. The top tier, where the lettuce leaves and baby had been the day before, was empty.

Since her dad's nine-headed assistant, Ms. Hydra, was busy over by the far wall and hadn't noticed her arrival, Athena didn't stop and sign in before visiting her dad, like students were supposed to. Instead she slipped past the assistant and made for Zeus's office a dozen steps away. As was often the case, his office door hung crazily from its one upper hinge. He didn't know his own strength and regularly slammed it so hard that it broke.

There was a strange sound coming from his office, like doves cooing off-key. *Creak!* She pulled the door partly open and peeked inside. Zeus was there, all right. He was bent over a crib beside his desk, cooing to Hebe! Apparently he'd completely forgotten about his practice with his *older* daughter.

His attention all on the baby, he didn't notice Athena. "Goochie, goochie goo! Who's Daddy's favorite girl?" he said, making silly faces at Hebe.

What? Athena froze, her feelings totally wounded.

Since she'd come to MOA, he had always called her "Theeny, my brainiest, most favorite daughter in the whole wide universe." Well, it looked like Hebe was his favorite now! She glared at the crib, wishing the baby had never appeared in that fountain.

A tiny hand reached out and grabbed Zeus's beard. When he tried to pull away, the baby started crying.

But he only laughed. "Hey! All that crying and beard-tugging is going to give me a headache. Not as humongous as the horrible headaches your big sister used to give me, though!" he said. Then he went crazy laughing in his usual big booming way, as if he'd just made a hilarious joke.

What was that supposed to mean? When had she given him a headache? If anything, he was the one who gave *her* a headache sometimes.

Because having Zeus as a dad wasn't easy. He could be loud and corny and embarrassing. And when electricity shot from his fingertips whenever he got angry or excited, he sometimes accidentally zapped her, her friends, and even her crush, Heracles. In spite of that, she truly admired and adored her dad. He'd made no secret of the fact that he was mega-proud of her too. But now Hebe had come along and stolen his fatherly affection. It wasn't fair!

"Hey, Theeny!" Zeus said casually, having noticed her at last. "You know . . . I was thinking. Let's make that Greek Fest next weekend a celebration in Hebe's honor. What do you say?"

There were many things Athena wanted to say about that idea. Mostly that no, it was *not* a good one! She had worked hard to organize the festival in Athens, the city named in *her* honor. And now her

79

dad wanted to turn the festival into one that honored this baby interloper?

When she said nothing, Zeus acted as if the matter were already settled. "Good. I knew you'd agree." Not even seeming to care that he'd missed their training session, he switched to his new favorite subject—making Hebe happy.

"Hand me that toy, will you?" he asked Athena. "It's Hebe's favorite."

Athena set down the bag she carried. The sword she'd bought yesterday was inside it. As she moved farther into her dad's office, her eyes went wide in surprise. His floor used to be cluttered with half-read scrollazines; old art projects; exercise equip-ment, including file cabinets he used as barbells; board games; maps; and empty bottles of Zeus Juice.

Recently he'd cleaned all that up, though. And he'd

donated much of his junk—or artifacts and artwork, as he liked to call it—to a museum that a student named Calliope had created as a class project. But now the office was a total mess again, a jumble of baby bottles, toys, bibs, baby outfits, and pacifiers.

Athena handed him the toy squeak doll he'd gestured to. Only, instead of giving the toy to the baby, he started playing with it himself, squeezing it to make it talk.

Squeak! "Necessity is the mother of invention," said the doll. Zeus let out a high-pitched giggle at this, that sounded totally unlike him. *Squeak!* "True friendship can exist only between equals." *Squeak!* "Always be kind, for everyone is fighting a hard battle."

That doll was squeaking out quotes by the philosopher Plato! Zeus knew that Plato was one of Athena's very favorite authors. To her it seemed kind of a betrayal that he was sharing the philosopher's words with Hebe. She was too young to understand them, anyway!

"Hello?" someone called from the outer office. A head wearing a winged cap poked in around Zeus's door. It was Hermes, the messenger god who flew all over the various realms delivering packages and urgent messages in his chariot. He'd even brought Athena here to Mount Olympus after Zeus had first summoned her from Triton to attend the Academy.

"Just dropped off a bag of mail on Ms. Hydra's desk," Hermes informed them.

"Uh-huh, good," Zeus replied, distracted. His attention was on two dolls now—the Plato one and another one that looked like the philosopher Socrates. He held both dolls in his meaty fists and perched them on the edge of Hebe's crib. Then he moved them around to mimic some kind of battle, pitting Plato against the other doll. In Athena's view, having them fight made no sense. Everyone knew that Plato was Socrates' prize student in real life!

"You okay?" Hermes asked Athena, coming to stand beside her. He was holding a cup of water and sipping from it.

"Mm-hmm," she mumbled, trying not to look as upset and confused as she felt at the moment.

"Well, there's something for you in the mail I just delivered," Hermes told her, gesturing outside Zeus's office door. Her dad didn't even look up when she grabbed her sword bag and followed Hermes out the door, returning to the main office.

All nine of Ms. Hydra's heads, each a different color, were still intent on whatever they were doing over by the wall. She hadn't yet bothered to open the bag of mail on her desk. And none of her heads looked over as Hermes and Athena approached her. What was up?

Athena's eyes practically popped out when she finally saw what Ms. Hydra was doing—coloring with ink pens on the wall! Since the assistant had nine heads but only two hands to hold the pens, the heads had begun arguing over which colors to use. Each favored their own matching color.

"I say we draw a yellow sun with a happy face," said her cheerful yellow head.

"That's lame. We should draw a big, green monster like Typhon," her grumpy green head put in.

"No. It's my turn to choose, and I want to make a purple flower!" argued her impatient purple head.

"Ah-hah! Here they are." Hermes had been digging through his mailbag and now pulled out a

84

bundle of letterscrolls. Sheepishly he held them out to Athena.

She went over to get them and saw right off that the return address was the same on all six letter-scrolls. "Pallas sent me all these at once?"

"Um, not exactly. They're dated over the past six weeks. I'd misplaced them in my chariot and just found them," Hermes told her. "Sorry about that."

Although she'd been majorly busy lately, in the back of her mind, Athena had kind of been wonder-ing why she hadn't heard from her Triton pal in a while. Her thoughts on her own troubles now, she just nodded and stuffed the letters into her bag, alongside her sword.

"Think I'll take another sip for the road," said Hermes, going over to dip his cup into the fountain.

"Zeus brought that thing here for the baby," Ms. Hydra's grumpy green head turned around briefly to inform them. "It's in the way, if you ask me, but Hebe likes the sound of its bubbling water. It soothes her to sleep."

"Yeah, and everything's got to be about the baby now," murmured Athena, feeling as grumpy as the green head always acted.

Ms. Hydra's sympathetic blue head swung her way. "You okay?" But before Athena could reply, the head got distracted and went back to arguing with the other heads about what to draw and what colors to use.

A moment later Hermes departed, so Athena did too. Still in her battle gear, she found a stone bench along the hall wall and sat down. *Clank!* Her mind was on her troubles, so she wasn't ready to return to her dorm room. Her roommate, Pandora, was probably there. That curious girl was always full of questions. Normally that was fine, but Athena wasn't really in the mood to answer them right now.

Her gaze fell on the half dozen letterscrolls Hermes had given her. After setting them in her lap, she picked up the first one, unrolled it, and began to read.

Pallas had written that she was making lots of friends. Doing really well. Having a blast at Triton Junior High and enjoying being part of the Cheer Blades team. Sounded like she hardly missed Athena at all, in fact. Athena's heart sank. This wasn't the best time for her to hear about how much fun Pallas was having without her. Not when she was feeling so unneeded already.

She quickly read through the next four letters,

feeling a little better when she noticed how Pallas had said something funny or personal in each one. Things such as, "Hope you're not having trouble keeping up with your studies. Ha-ha, as if." And, "You're so brainy, I'm sure you already know this, but . . ."

That was the friend she knew. Back when Athena had been teased at TJH for her growing immortal powers (which no one had understood), Pallas had always stuck up for her and encouraged her too.

Athena ran the tip of her finger over Pallas's sign-off at the end of the letter. She signed all her letters the same way—*Your Pal*.

Yes, Pallas *was* a pal. A good one. And Athena missed her, despite having made new friends.

One of Pallas's letters had said she'd been baby-sitting to earn money. Athena sat up straighter. *Snap!*

The letterscroll rolled itself up on her lap. So her old friend must have learned something about babies by now. She tapped the letterscroll against her knee, thinking.

Maybe Pallas would be the perfect friend to offer some helpful advice about this whole new baby business! If only Athena had time to go visit Triton and talk to her. But there was too much to do, with homework and the festival and all that. Instead she would write to Pallas and ask her to come visit MOA. Pallas was easy to talk to and always had good ideas. Maybe she'd even have ideas on how Athena could win back Zeus's favor!

Athena was just about to read Pallas's last letter, which appeared to be some kind of invitation, when Hera ran past her toward the office.

"Hi, Hera," Athena said. "Wow, you look kind

of . . . different." Usually her stepmom's blond hair was styled high on her head in a sophisticated way that Athena had always admired. Now Hera was wearing it in two scraggly, lopsided ponytails. And there wasn't any makeup on her face either.

"Thanks!" Hera giggled, waggling her fingers in a girlish hello. "I'm here to see Zeus," she announced. Without waiting for a reply, she pushed on into the office.

Athena stared after her in surprise. Then something clicked. Ye gods! Aphrodite must've already gotten started on those youthful makeovers for teachers that she'd talked about for Beauty-ology class. Only Hera's makeover wasn't especially successful, in Athena's humble opinion!

5

Training

Pallas

IT WAS SUNDAY AFTERNOON, AND PALLAS AND Eurynome stood on the grassy athletic field next to the chariot track outside Triton Junior High. Each of them held a sports bag. With their free hands they tried to keep their long hair from tangling in the wind being stirred up by a flying chariot that was coming in for a landing. Bearing the IM logo, it was part of the fleet whose magic worked for both mortals and immortals.

When the two-seater touched down, Achilles and Agamemnon jumped out and greeted the girls. This would be their first practice together. If all went well, Pallas hoped to learn some useful tips and strategies that would improve her chances in the Greek Fest competition. And maybe help her wow Athena, too. If her friend *had* witnessed Pallas's mess-up at the IM with her dad's sword, she would quickly realize it had only been a onetime mistake.

Achilles had come up to Eurynome. "So I guess I'll be your—," he started to say to her.

"Dibs on Eurynome," Agamemnon butted in quickly. "Your champion will be her." He pointed at Pallas.

"No problem," said Achilles. He smiled over at

Pallas. Something about his sweet, almost shy expression made her suddenly wonder if he had anticipated that Agamemnon would steal his first choice of trainee. Did that mean Achilles had just pulled a trick on his friend so that Achilles and Pallas would wind up paired? Her cheeks went pink at the thought.

"C'mon, Eurynome. See ya, Dip," Agamemnon told Achilles.

Achilles nodded. "Later." While Agamemnon took Eurynome to find a practice area, Pallas and Achilles walked in the opposite direction, looking for a separate flat open space to train in.

"Why does he call you 'Dip'?" Pallas asked Achilles as they walked. It seemed like a hurtful nickname to her.

Achilles jerked his head upward, flipping his bangs out of his eyes, before he grinned over at her.

"Because my mom dipped me into the River Styx when I was a baby. It made me kind of invincible."

"Wow! Cool," said Pallas, impressed. Usually only immortals were invincible. They could never die and had a substance called ichor flowing in their veins instead of blood.

"Comes in handy during swordplay, that's for sure," said Achilles. Stopping in a flat practice area, they both dropped their sports bags onto the ground. Promptly Achilles went down on one knee and began pulling equipment out of his bag.

"So how is this festival competition actually going to work? Do you know?" Pallas asked, watching him. "I mean, is everyone in the same arena or what?"

"No, there'll be separate arenas for each pair. I read the list of rules last night. Each competitor will be assigned a character from a particular battle and then will reenact that battle in a bout." He pulled out two fancy shields that bore the red-and-black insignia of his school, then went on. "Your skill in the swordfight will be scored and will determine the winner."

"So if I win a round, I'll advance to more rounds against other winners?"

Achilles nodded, handing her one of the shields. "And in the end the two best competitors will be pitted against each other, and a grand prize winner will be chosen."

"That'll be me!" Pallas said. She was half-joking, but she also knew that confidence was half the battle. Grinning, she lifted the shield and punched it high overhead as if in victory.

Overhearing, Eurynome did the same with the shield she held and called out, "You wish!"

Pallas waved at her, and they both laughed. The

two boys frowned and moved Pallas and Eurynome to practice areas that were farther apart. These guys were friends, but they obviously took their training seriously. She guessed they didn't want her and Eurynome fooling around during practices. They each considered the girl they were working with to be their champion and wanted her to shine the brightest in the competition.

"Okay, so where's your sword?" Achilles asked her when they reached a new spot.

"I brought two." Pallas bent and opened her sports bag. First she whipped out her dad's sword in one hand. Then she pulled out a banged-up sword she'd gotten from school—the kind newbie swordplayers used—in her other. Her dad's was iron, and the school one was bronze. Both were fairly bendable metals, unfortunately.

Achilles' eyes widened in horror at the sight of the awful swords, but at least he didn't say anything mean.

She grinned at him. "So you can see why I want to win that sword on the poster."

He nodded, grinning back. "Yeah. Definitely. But sheathe your blades. Today we'll practice with these." He whipped out two wooden swords from his bag.

"*Wood* swords?" she scoffed, taking the one he handed her and making an *ick* face. "These are for babies. I thought you were invincible. Which means I couldn't accidentally hurt you if we use real blades, right?"

"But I could hurt you. And even wood swords can result in bruises or cuts. Pain from hits too. In the real competition all the blades will be bespelled to prevent lethal injury, though."

She opened her mouth to interrupt.

"I'm not doubting your skills," he assured her before she could speak. "I'd even bet you could teach me a thing or two. But you can learn from me, too. I've been trained by immortals who've seen real combat with giants, beasts, and other immortals. So let's do things my way for now."

"Okay," said Pallas. What he'd said made sense. She was glad he wasn't all pompous or acting like a know-it-all at least. When she glanced over at Eurynome, her friend did not look happy. Pallas had a feeling Agamemnon was not going to prove as tactful or patient a teacher as Achilles.

"Take your starting position," instructed Achilles.

Pallas did, right arm bent with the shield clasped in her right hand. She gripped the hilt of her wooden sword in her left fist. The hilt consisted of a handle and a short metal bar called a cross guard, meant to protect her hand. The sword's blade was long and flat, but its end was blunt, not pointed.

"Wooden swords just feel so . . . baby," she couldn't help complaining. "We use these in first grade here at my school."

He ignored her complaint and said, "You're left-handed, huh? Let me see your grip."

She moved her shield a bit to show him how she held the sword, with her fingers and thumb gripping the handle. He eyed her hand critically, then hooked her forefinger in a different position through the protective ring that extended out from the cross guard.

For a second they were practically holding hands! *Whoa, where had that thought come from?* Usually, she didn't think much about boys at all. Pallas found herself flushing again and hoped he hadn't noticed. She wasn't starting to crush on this boy, was she? She shook off the thought. No, they were here to practice.

"That's a better hold. It'll give you more control of the blade," Achilles approved. "Now show me your stance again."

With her left arm bent, Pallas held the sword so its point was higher than the handle. In her right hand she clasped the shield, holding it slightly out from her body as protection.

"Good," he pronounced. He grabbed a shield and sword and took his stance across from her. "Ready? On guard!"

They went on the attack with their blades, making cutting and thrusting moves. Pallas lunged. *Thunk!* Their wood swords made contact.

"Remember, it's not just about skill," Achilles

cautioned her at one point. "It's about theatrics. During the competition, try to create the illusion of danger even when you know you can't be killed by the bespelled swords. Perform flourishes. Excite the crowd. That could discourage your opponent and help you win points. Now, let's begin again."

"Okay, good tip, thanks," replied Pallas. This time she varied her approaches. She swung her left hand, making cuts toward the left and right of her opponent. Sometimes she thrust out with the flat of her blade, and other times with its edge. Seeing an opening, she swung her sword hard, pivoting her elbow in a circular movement. Catching Achilles unawares, she struck his shoulder. He jerked away, stumbling in surprise.

"Sorry," she said, hoping she hadn't injured him.

"Don't be," he said. "That was amazing." Then

he did that hair-flicking thing again to shake his bangs out of his eyes. Eyes that were a sparkly green. "Obviously I underestimated your ability. Let's keep on."

Achilles was actually kind of cute, she decided. Way nicer than he'd seemed back at the IM, too. And less bossy than his friend for sure.

She glanced over at Eurynome and Agamemnon again. They were sparring, but judging from Eurynome's frown, Pallas guessed her friend wasn't thinking good thoughts about her own coach. Far from it. As Achilles and Pallas continued doing drills, she came to appreciate his knowledge and skill. He had all sorts of small suggestions that added up to a big help, like that change in her grip. It was giving her more directional control over the swing of her blade.

In the middle of a swing, a strange glittery breeze suddenly blew past her face, carrying a rolled-up piece of papyrus. *A message for Pallas from Mount Olympus!* the wind howled.

"I'm Pallas," she called, losing focus on the bout for a second.

"Gotcha!" Achilles announced softly.

Her eyes widened as she gazed down at the point of his sword. It was planted dead center at her chest. "I guess I'm glad you suggested wood swords after all," she told him.

Apparently Agamemnon had been watching from across the lawn. He started to laugh. "Oops! You're dead!"

Eurynome said something to him. He shrugged but continued to chuckle.

"Meanie," Pallas muttered under her breath.

Achilles laughed in a good-humored way and withdrew his blade. "You got distracted. Understandable. Letterscrolls from immortals don't arrive every day."

"True!" Hastily Pallas dropped her sword and chased down the scroll, which was bouncing along the ground, still blown by the breeze. She unrolled it. It was from Athena! A thrill shot through her as she scanned it:

I need you, Pal. Let me know if you can come to MOA today, and I'll send one of the MOA chariots.

~ Athena

Athena *needed* her? *Humph.* Pallas couldn't help feeling a little miffed. Where had Athena been when *she* had needed *her* yesterday and in recent weeks, huh? Athena shouldn't just think that Pallas would jump whenever she bothered to call. "Maybe I'm busy," she grumbled.

Achilles walked over. "Problem?"

"Nuh-uh. Not really." Pallas rolled up Athena's invitation and dropped it into her sports bag.

"Listen," Achilles said, sounding more serious. "You'll lose the competition for sure if you get distracted in a real battle like you did back there."

"I'll never be in a *real* battle," said Pallas, meaning a war.

"I meant in a real competition battle," said Achilles. "We're a team, both in this to win it. You need a new sword, obviously. But the truth is . . ." He lowered his voice, then continued. "I want Briseis back from Agamemnon. And he wants that grand prize sword. So I figure if you win the prize sword for me, I can trade it to him for what I want."

"And if Eurynome or someone else wins the prize instead?" Both girls planned do their best.

"Well, you and I are going to train our hardest out here so that that won't happen. Deal?"

"Sure." She scrunched her face in confusion. "Only, why'd you give Briseis to Agamemnon to begin with if that was the sword you really wanted?"

Achilles brushed the grass with the tip of his wooden sword. "It's complicated," he said. "Agamemnon can get supercompetitive and jealous, especially when it comes to my whole invincible thing. It's my fault—I shouldn't have let him see how much I wanted that sword. Usually I'm more careful. I know I'm making him sound bad to you, and he can be a bully sometimes. But I've known him forever and he has stuck by me when I needed him in the past. I don't ditch my friends."

She cocked her head at him. "What kind of a friend leads you into trouble? I overheard him say you were on suspension from swordplay competition, and I'm betting whatever happened was his fault."

Achilles shrugged. "Yeah, long story. There was this cool spear he liked—the only one of the new Clytemnestra brand at our school. Another guy claimed it to use in a gym class competition and scored better than him. Let's just say trouble ensued. The upshot was that we all got temporarily suspended for bad sportsmanship."

Pallas raised her eyebrows but didn't say anything. It wasn't her business to tell him that his best bud was kind of rotten. "I'll be more careful about not getting distracted in the real bouts. Promise," she told him.

Taking her position, she faced off with Achilles again, her blade and shield at the ready. "On guard!"

she warned with fierce determination. The rest of the afternoon passed swiftly as both teams worked industriously. By the time they'd finished, Pallas was sweating, her breath coming in hard gasps.

"Good work, champ," Achilles told her, looking pleased.

"Thanks, Coach," she said, grinning at him.

As the boys got ready to leave, Achilles asked Agamemnon, "How did it go?"

"Eurynome needs work, but I'm bringing her up to speed." Agamemnon glanced over at the two girls. "Right, Eurynome?"

Eurynome shrugged and muttered something under her breath.

"At least she didn't almost wind up a shish kebab at the end of my sword like Pallas did on yours," Agamemnon went on, not seeming to care that he was being kind of insulting to his friend and to Eurynome both, in Pallas's opinion.

However, when Agamemnon laughed at his own joke, Achilles just smiled and clapped him on the back. Though Pallas couldn't understand why Achilles remained friends with the guy, she supposed it was commendable that he stuck by his bud, even if Agamemnon *was* a selfish bully.

After the boys lifted off for the IM, the girls began to head home on foot. "Wow! That was some workout," Pallas remarked to Eurynome.

"Yeah." Eurynome's face was tight and her voice quiet.

"You okay?" Pallas asked her.

"Just tired. Of Agamemnon." She glanced at Pallas and rolled her eyes. They both laughed. "I'm learning a lot, but he's really full of himself. I've decided not to let it get to me, though. I simply nod and smile. He probably thinks that means I agree with everything he says."

Pallas laughed again. "Probably."

Eurynome glanced at Pallas's bag as the two girls neared their village. "So that letterscroll you got. I'm guessing it came from Athena since you don't really know any other immortals and they're the ones who send them."

Pallas nodded and then told Eurynome about the invitation to visit MOA and her decision not to go. "I'm a little mad that she seems to think I should always be at her beck and call." Then Pallas sighed and admitted softly, "I do miss her, though. Every now and then something interesting or just silly will happen, and I wish I could tell her. Or I think of something that would make her laugh, but I can't tell her that, either. And then I get sad." The words just poured out, before she could stop them.

"Aw, I'm sorry," Eurynome empathized, leaning sideways to gently bump Pallas's shoulder with her own. "And I know what you mean. I miss my BFF back at my old school too."

Pallas looked at her in surprise. She had never considered that Eurynome might have a BFF that Pallas knew nothing about. She hadn't really noticed Eurynome when she had first come to Triton. Because Athena had still been around.

"I guess you can understand what I'm going through, then," said Pallas.

"Yeah, but my BFF wasn't a goddessgirl," Eurynome noted. "That's got to make it extra hard for you. Immortals are so amazing and out of reach, with tons of friends and admirers. It's not easy to compete for her attention, right?"

"Exactly," said Pallas, pleased that Eurynome "got" it. "There are constant reminders of her success in *Teen Scrollazine*. I'm proud of her, don't get me wrong. Still, I can't help feeling abandoned. It's like I just get scraps of Athena now, when I used to have all of her."

"You have me, though," Eurynome said gently.

Pallas nodded. *But no one will ever replace Athena,* she thought. She hoped Eurynome knew that, because Pallas wouldn't want Eurynome to get her hopes up about them becoming BFFs.

Yet lately Pallas *had* been thinking that Eurynome was becoming a really, really good friend. They did have fun doing stuff together, and they both loved Cheer Blades. Athena had liked swordplay too, but not as much as Eurynome did.

Although Pallas really liked Eurynome, she still missed Athena too much to let anyone get as close to her as Athena had always been. And even though she knew it was wishful thinking and pretty unlikely, in her heart she secretly kept hoping that someday Athena would move back to Triton and everything would go back to how it used to be.

6

The Big Day

Athena

IT WAS SATURDAY A WEEK LATER, ON THE morning of the Greek Fest. Athena tiptoed around her shadowy dorm room, trying not to wake Pandora since the sun wasn't even up yet. She sighed, hunting through her closet for her lucky aegis, a large collar with a shield attached that protected her chest. Where was it?

Then she remembered. Oh yeah, her dad had borrowed it last week for a ceremony at one of the many temples dedicated to him. He'd promised to return it to her, but he'd gotten a little distracted since then with the arrival of Hebe. Athena needed it today, though, for the reenactment competition. Could she depend on him to bring it? She'd have to, because there was no time to go find him right now. He was probably asleep anyway, like Pandora.

Quickly Athena went over to her desk and sent Zeus a messagescroll reminding him to bring the aegis to the festival this morning. She used lots of exclamation points to emphasize how important this was. Leaning out her window, she released the scroll on a magic breeze that would take it to him.

She crossed her fingers that the message would do the trick and Zeus wouldn't forget like he'd forgotten their sword practice. He was acting pretty irresponsible lately, and goofy, too. Earlier in the week she'd seen him in his office, swinging his arms like a monkey and jumping from his desk to the chairs to make Hebe giggle. It was like all he wanted to do lately was play.

Athena pulled a shirt of armor from her closet and slipped it over her head just in case he forgot the aegis despite her reminder. The armor was blue and gold, which matched the chiton she wore underneath. She fastened on gold wristbands and her owl earrings, hoping they would lend her wisdom today. Finally she slipped on golden sandals and shin guards. She smiled at her image in the closet door mirror, thinking Aphrodite would likely approve. She looked ready for battle, yet chic!

A dog began barking down the hall. It had to be

one of Artemis's dogs, since hers were the only dogs in the dorm. Athena glanced at Pandora, hoping the barking wouldn't wake her. A door closed and she heard footsteps and the click of doggie toenails out in the hall. Artemis must be taking her hounds outside for an early morning run.

Athena bent to reach under her bed for the sword she'd bought at Mighty Fighty. She hadn't fastened one of her wristbands properly, and it fell off to the floor. *Clink!*

Abruptly Pandora sat up in bed and pushed back a strand of blue-streaked hair that had fallen over one eye. It boinged back into its usual question-mark shape. "Going somewhere?" she asked sleepily.

"Greek Fest today, remember?" replied Athena. Standing with the sword, she fastened the wristband correctly this time.

Pandora yawned. "Oh? What time is it?"

"Five," said Athena.

"In the morning? Are you crazy? That's way too early for me, but I'll be there when the gates open, okay? See you later?"

"Sure, go back to sleep."

Pandora took her advice, snuggled in her covers, and went back to snoozing. Meanwhile, Athena headed out of the dorm in the dark and flew on winged sandals down to Athens. She landed at her temple complex just as the sunrise lit the horizon pink.

She and her three BFFs had spent every afternoon here this week setting things up, but there were still many details that needed to be taken care of. Quickly Athena pulled out her checklist and got busy, darting here and there to make sure things were in order.

Over the next few hours her friends arrived to help out. Persephone was in charge of decorations and had gathered enormous bouquets of irises, daffodils, chrysanthemums, and daisies. She placed them in urns around the perimeter of Athena's main temple, the Parthenon, and at the base of its front steps.

"That looks mega-amazing," Athena complimented her as she was walking by.

Just then Artemis came out of the temple carrying an upside-down helmet. It was an oversize one that Athena recognized as belonging to Mr. Cyclops, their oversize Hero-ology teacher.

"Here you go: the first sixty-four scrolls. I wrote out the name of a historical battle and the name of a person who fought in that battle on every scroll, and then Aphrodite tied a ribbon around each one, see?"

Artemis tilted the big helmet toward the other two goddessgirls, showing them that it was full of small beribboned papyrus scrolls.

As Athena nodded her approval, Persephone clasped her hands in delight. "They're so cute! So how's this all going to work?"

Though the contest had originally been Zeus's idea, Athena was one who had mostly figured out how to organize it. "We start with sixty-four entrants, who'll each get one of the scrolls in this helmet, and then compete in pairs. The victors in this round will receive another scroll and move on to a second bout," she explained.

"There are only two of each ribbon design," Artemis added. "Matching ribbons mean match-ups of two opponents who once fought each other in a famous battle."

Reaching into the helmet, Athena pulled out the only two scrolls tied with red-and-white polka-dot ribbons. "So a pair of competitors will get these two scrolls today. They'll each represent one of the two historical opponents in a battle and reenact that swordfight. Six rounds of reenactments will gradually narrow the field of sixty-four to a single winner."

"I get it," said Persephone. "So sixty-four narrows to thirty-two, then sixteen, then eight, then four, then the final two."

The very last battle would be the highlight of the day, and Athena was determined to make it all the way to that final competition—and win it! She wanted to make Zeus and Hera proud. Maybe then they'd remember who their favorite daughter was! (Hint: Not Hebe!)

7

Greek Fest

Pallas

It was Saturday, the morning of the Greek

Fest in Athens. Pallas, Eurynome, and a chariot full of

excited villagers from Triton were traveling through

the air toward a complex of buildings on a hill known

as the acropolis, which was the site of the festival.

"Wow! Look!" shouted a young boy, pointing to the

many colorful flags that marked the festival's location.

So far, Pallas had managed to keep her dad from discovering that she'd mangled his sword. She had brought it along today in hopes of speaking to the godboy, Hephaestus, about fixing it in his forge. However, she would leave it in the chariot till she found him. Agamemnon and Achilles had promised to meet and lend their swords to Eurynome and her before the reenactments began, and she wouldn't be able to carry *two* swords in the sheath at her side.

The minute the chariot landed, everyone stepped out and took off up the hill to Athena's greatest temple, the Parthenon. Eurynome gazed with big eyes at the rectangular building. "It's enormous!" she exclaimed.

Pallas nodded, feeling awed. The inside of the temple was just as amazing. "Wow!" she breathed as they toured it. Just think, a whole temple dedicated to her BFF. There was even a huge statue of Athena at the far end.

For twelve years they'd lived together like sisters back in Triton, just doing everyday stuff. Who would have ever dreamed that Athena would one day have a magnificent temple like this? In spite of everything she'd been feeling lately, in this moment Pallas felt proud of her friend. Would they finally run into each other today? What would they say? Would Athena be happy to see her?

Outside the temple again, she and Eurynome began to walk around it. Forty-six fluted Doric columns surrounded its outer edge. (She counted!) Painted sculptures showing scenes from an Athenian festival decorated the top of the temple's outer walls in bright blue, red, gold, and white.

A clanking sound accompanied the girls as they

walked, since they'd both worn armored shirts in preparation for the competition. "This armor sure is noisy," noted Eurynome.

"Bulky, too," said Pallas, "but I'm getting used to it." Although contestants were required to wear armor in the battles, it was more for show than in case of accidents. After all, their blades would be bespelled to protect them all.

Mortals and immortals from every land had been invited here today. And there would be many other events and activities besides the battle reenactments.

Clank! Clank! The girls stepped over to a low wall just beyond the Parthenon and peered down at the amphitheater far below, where those battle reenactments would be held later in the day. For now an entertaining dramatic play called *The Iliad*, written by a popular teenage boy author named Homer, was being performed in the theater.

As Pallas and Eurynome strolled around the grounds outside the temple, they passed booths that had been set up in anticipation of the day's event. Some were small shops selling food or trinkets, and the girls each bought a little something. There were game booths too, such as the ever-popular Dunk the Immortal.

Eurynome grabbed Pallas's arm in excitement. "Ooh! Look! Is that Poseidon sitting on the dunking seat?"

Pallas looked over and nodded. A long line of mortals and immortals snaked up to the booth. Apparently lots of people were hoping to dunk the famous godboy of the sea. When Pallas had gone to MOA to visit Athena that one time, she'd been mega-excited to see Poseidon too.

"I met him when I slept over at MOA," Pallas informed Eurynome. "He's really cute but kind of drippy."

They clanked past more booths. The strongman one featured Athena's crush, Heracles, who was wearing his trademark lion-skin cape. *CRUNCH!* Wielding his enormous club, time after time he smashed boulders twice his size to delight his audience. Amazed at this show of strength, the crowd that had gathered around him applauded and cheered.

Pallas had never actually met Heracles, so now she studied him with interest. Athena had said she'd helped him with some jobs called labors a while back. Since Athena was so brainy, it was kind of surprising that she would crush on someone so brawny. Not that brains and brawn couldn't ever go together, of course. Zeus had big muscles. And he was so smart that he was King of the Gods! But still.

The girls strolled on, taking everything in. One of the booths in the art area soon caught their attention.

"Hey, look at those cutout thingies," said Pallas, nudging Eurynome. She pointed at a group of life-size painted images of immortals that stood scattered around a grassy area, like big paper dolls. Only these were made of flat pieces of wood. An oval section had been cut out of each where the immortal's face would normally be.

"You need a ticket," a boy informed them in a superior tone. It was Agamemnon, waving a ticket he'd bought under their noses, and Achilles was with him. "And those *cutout thingies* are called stand-ins, by the way."

"That's because you stand in back of them and

poke your head through the hole where the face should be," Achilles explained. "And an artist draws your picture so you look like you're the immortal. Fun, huh?" He was also holding a ticket.

While they all watched a bunch of people poking their heads through the holes in the stand-ins, the two boys unsheathed their swords and passed them to the girls. These were the swords Eurynome and Pallas would use for the reenactments today. Both were shiny, straight, and true and of better quality than any the girls had ever owned or used.

"Nice," said Eurynome, admiring Agamemnon's sword, which Achilles had named Briseis.

"Here you go," Achilles told Pallas as he gave her *his* sword. "Meet Evgenís."

"You named your sword 'Noble'?" she asked him, smiling.

"Agamemnon named it that, actually," Achilles told her.

"Hmm. Well, I still like the name in spite of that," she half-joked. She spoke quietly, so only Achilles would hear, and he laughed.

As both girls sheathed their borrowed swords in the scabbards at their sides, Eurynome nodded in the direction of the stand-ins. "Those look like fun. Want to do it?" she asked Pallas.

Pallas agreed readily. After waving bye to the boys, they went to buy tickets.

"Right," said the man in charge of the sales booth. "Just choose your favorite immortal cutout, and the artist assigned to it will draw you a ten-by-twelve-inch caricature of your face on the immortal's body." He gestured toward the nearest artist. She was drawing a picture of Agamemnon, who was now posing in the cutout of Zeus.

Farther off, Achilles went to stand in the only other available cutout at the moment—Hera. He smiled goofily, batting his eyelashes at the small crowd gathering around the artist who was drawing him. The two girls joined that crowd and watched the artist sketch Achilles wearing a stylish chiton, with beautiful blond hair styled atop his head. It was hilarious!

"Achilles is a *girrrrl*!" Agamemnon sing-songed in a voice that floated out across the lawn.

"Smart choice!" Heracles yelled to Achilles from over at the strongman booth. "If you ever need a disguise, it's perfect, mortal-dude!"

Agamemnon frowned, but Pallas grinned. She

admired Achilles for not being afraid to act silly!

"Agamemnon probably wishes now that he'd thought of posing in the Hera cutout himself," said Eurynome, giggling.

"Yeah," Pallas agreed. "Typical. It was pretty nice of Heracles to stick up for Achilles like that, though." Athena had chosen her crush well, it seemed.

"C'mon, let's do this," Eurynome told Pallas. Breaking away from the crowd around Achilles, she dashed to stand in line for the Aphrodite cutout. Pallas darted in the other direction to pose in the Athena one. These two goddessgirls were very popular, and they had to wait to take their turns. But it was worth it!

Pallas planned to hang her new portrait on her bedroom wall once she was home again. For now she tucked it into the cross-body bag she'd bought at a crafts booth earlier.

The girls had come full circle around the Parthenon, when suddenly a clear voice rang out from the top of the Parthenon steps. Pallas looked over to see Athena standing there!

"Mortals and immortals! Welcome to the Greek Fest!" Athena greeted everyone, smiling out at the crowds. "My father, Zeus, was supposed to make this announcement. However, he has been, um, delayed." Her smile wilted briefly, but then sprang to life again as she continued. "So anyway, I want to thank you all for coming. I hope you'll visit the booths and explore the acropolis. Your purchase of game tickets, food, and arts and crafts at this event will go to support the building of the new Cynosarges Community Center for the people of Athens."

Athena paused as cheers rose briefly at that announcement, and then she went on. "The center

133

will feature gardens, fruit orchards, and olive groves for all to enjoy, plus a gymnasium for athletic training in skills including boxing, wrestling, and sword-fighting. Speaking of which, I hope everyone's excited about the battle reenactments. I know I am!" Here, she grinned, and more cheers sounded.

Then everyone listened closely as Athena continued. "The reenactments will be held at three locations around the acropolis—arenas A, B, and C—beginning in two hours and continuing throughout the day. The sixth, final battle between the last two remaining contestants will be held in the Theatre of Dionysus, and it's sure to be thrilling. Because no matter how the real battles turned out, anyone can win today. There's a big stage and plenty of seats, so come join in the fun, cheer for your favorites, and see who claims final victory to win this amazing sword!"

At this, the crowd went wild with anticipation and began looking around for the sword.

On cue the goddessgirls Aphrodite and Persephone brought forth the grand prize sword that Pallas had seen on the poster. At the sight of the gleaming blade with its ruby jewel, the crowd applauded.

The goddessgirl Artemis moved up the steps to join Athena and hold up a large golden helmet upside down. "All sixty-four of those signed up for the sword reenactments may come forward now to receive their first sets of scrolls with assignments for bouts from this helmet," she instructed. "For later bouts, scrolls will be available at the three arenas throughout the day leading up to the final event."

Those who had entered the competition, including Eurynome and Pallas, began to form a line. As they shuffled toward Artemis and the helmet, Eurynome leaned over to Pallas and whispered, "Who do you think the new community center will be dedicated to?"

"Probably an immortal. Maybe Athena herself," said Pallas. While they waited in line, she watched Athena smoothly answering questions from the throng of fans and attendees who surrounded her now. She seemed incredibly comfortable being in charge of everything.

The line moved forward a bit, and a cloud of unhappiness and uncertainty settled over Pallas. This was a totally different Athena than she remembered. "Being a goddessgirl sure makes you confident," she murmured to Eurynome. "Athena is talking to teachers, goddessgirls, and even godboys like it's no big deal!" *I could never do that,* Pallas thought. How well did she even know Athena anymore?

"Yeah, and teachers and godboys aren't the easiest

people to talk to," Eurynome said in an admiring tone. "I've always liked Athena. I remember she was supernice to me when I first came to Triton Junior High. On my very first day she saw me in the hall looking kind of lost and showed me where my locker was."

Pallas's spirits lifted some. "That's Athena. Supernice." That much about her friend probably hadn't changed, she hoped.

When it was their turn, the two girls each pulled scrolls from the helmet, then hurried back down the steps to untie them. "I got the battle of the Amazon Penthesilea versus the Greek hero Makhaon," said Pallas after they left the line. "I'm playing Penthesilea. What'd you get?"

"The Trojan War. Paris versus Menelaus," said Eurynome. "I'm Paris of Troy. Hope things turn

137

out better for me than they did for him, since the Trojans lost."

"Just remember what Athena said," Pallas reminded her. "We can win in the reenactment even if our character lost in reality!"

"Good thing!" Eurynome stuck her scroll into her bag. Then she pulled out a small folded piece of papyrus. "Hey, I almost forgot. I got us both something at one of the artist's booths while you were still posing in the Athena cutout. For good luck in our competitions."

She pulled out a necklace with a purple *P* charm on it and handed it to Pallas. Then she showed Pallas a similar necklace with an *E* charm for "Eurynome." The *E* was red to match the red streaks in Eurynome's medium-brown hair. The purple *P* matched the color of the streaks in Pallas's hair.

"How sweet! Thanks," said Pallas, admiring it.

"I can use all the luck I can get today." Quickly she helped Eurynome clasp the red charm necklace around her neck.

As Eurynome was fastening the *P* charm necklace around Pallas's throat, Athena, Aphrodite, Artemis, and Persephone happened to walked by. On seeing Pallas, Athena came to an abrupt halt. "Pallas!" she yelled in a high-pitched, thrilled-sounding voice. Then she dashed over and enveloped Pallas in a hug, which wasn't easy to do, since both girls were wearing armor.

Afterward, feeling ecstatically happy, Pallas said hi to the other goddessgirls and quickly introduced Eurynome. Was it just her imagination, she wondered, or did a slight cloud come over Athena's face when she realized that Pallas had come to the festival with a friend? It disappeared quickly, though.

Athena's gaze went to the purple *P* necklace that

Pallas wore. "Love your charm!" she commented, her blue-gray eyes sparkling.

"It's kind of a good luck charm," Eurynome put in. "I bought it for her at one of the artist booths. You know, doing my part to support that new Cynosarges Center you were talking about a minute ago."

Uh-oh, Pallas thought. Would Athena think Eurynome's gift meant more than it really did, that it meant Eurynome had replaced Athena as Pallas's BFF? Of course, Athena and her three goddessgirl friends were all wearing their gold *GG* charm necklaces too. Which was kind of the same. Still, no way did Pallas want Athena to think she no longer considered Athena to be her one and only BFF. Nervous knots filled Pallas's stomach at the thought of her true BFF getting the wrong idea about Eurynome.

"Hmm. Too bad I didn't bring my good luck charm. But he's a little big to lug around," said Athena. Her eyes twinkled, and Pallas could tell she wasn't annoyed.

Pallas relaxed immediately at this reference to an inside joke. "Woody, you mean? Ha! I could just see you carrying him as a shield in one arm while you try to wield your sword with your other arm during the competitions."

"Woody would never work as a shield," said Athena.

"Or *wood he*?" Pallas replied quickly. Which made Athena crack up.

Suddenly they were both smiling, and it felt just like old times. Athena wasn't a hoity-toity goddess-girl. She was just *Athena*, Pallas's best pal.

"What's a 'wood he'?" asked Eurynome. She and

the other three goddessgirls were staring at the two old friends with bemused expressions.

"Woody is Athena's toy horse," Pallas explained. Then she told how as a little kid Athena had clung to the wooden horse whenever she was scared or needed some luck.

Artemis looked at Athena. "Oh, yeah. You brought him to MOA the day you enrolled, right?"

"Mm-hm, and Medusa teased you about him your first time in Hero-ology class, remember?" said Aphrodite.

Athena rolled her eyes comically. "How could I forget?"

Soon the girls began walking along as a group and moved on to other topics. The goddessgirls exclaimed over Pallas's and Eurynome's streaked hair, admiring it. Pallas had forgotten how nice these goddessgirls all were. And Eurynome was fitting right in. Mega-cool!

Hearing a splash and screeches of laughter, they arrived at the dunking booth just as Poseidon came up sputtering and soaked to the skin. "Who did that?" he growled, since it appeared that several mortals had been tossing balls at the same time.

The mortal who had successfully thrown the ball that had released the lever stopped laughing and now looked a little worried. So did the rest of the audience. Offending a godboy was never wise.

Then Poseidon unexpectedly grinned. "Gotcha!" he said, starting to laugh. He'd only been pretending to be angry!

A girl with turquoise hair appeared and stepped up beside the dunk tank to speak. Pallas and Eurynome craned their necks to get a better look at her.

"Hey! That's Amphitrite!" Eurynome whispered to Pallas, who nodded. Seeing Athena looking their way, Pallas added, "We read about her and you and those giants in *Teen Scrollazine*." Though Amphitrite walked while on land, she was actually a Nereid whose legs shape-shifted into a mermaid tail when she swam in the sea. She'd recently helped Athena find an herb that had prevented a hundred giants from taking over the world!

"Let's hear it for the godboy of the sea!" Amphitrite called out. "He's been working his *tail* off all morning to stay dry!"

Everyone laughed at her mermaid-inspired joke.

Smiling at Amphitrite, Poseidon climbed up to sit in the dunking seat once more. "Congratulations, mortal who dunked me! I now reward your success with a tribute." As he spoke, he caused water to shoot out of the tips of his three-pronged trident, sprinkling the crowd. Which of course made them laugh again as well as rush to get in line to buy more tickets to try their luck at dunking him once more.

Athena sighed reluctantly, looking at Pallas and the other four girls. "Sorry to bail on the fun, guys, but I'd better go. I need to check on how the other activities and events are going."

"Where's your dad?" asked Persephone, looking around.

"Yeah, I thought he was going to help you organize things today," said Artemis. "You'll get busy once the reenactments start, since you're in the competition. You can't oversee the festival too."

Before Athena could reply, the girls heard what sounded like little kids giggling. To their surprise, the giggling was actually coming from a bunch of grown-ups standing under some olive trees not far away.

"Huh?" said Athena. "What are my dad and Hera doing over there?"

"Look, they brought Hebe!" said Persephone.

"Who's Hebe?" Pallas asked, but everyone was too focused on the group of giggling grown-ups to answer her question.

8
Goofy Grown-Ups

Athena

RIGHT AWAY ATHENA SPOTTED HEBE CRADLED in Hera's arms. Hera was somewhat boisterously rocking the baby from side to side while feeding her from a baby bottle.

As for Zeus, he was crawling on his hands and knees around and around them, acting like some kind of muscular bearded baby himself. Hera apparently thought this was hilarious. So did the other grown-ups in the group under the trees, which included several MOA teachers all laughing their heads off.

Athena, however, did not find her dad's antics the least bit amusing. He was supposed to be helping with the fest! On the bright side, since he hadn't helped her make the greeting speech, he hadn't been able to proclaim the festival to be in Hebe's honor as he'd proposed.

"Oh, Zeus! You are sooo *craaazeee*!" Hera screeched just then in a high-pitched voice that hurt everyone's ears. Then she giggled again.

Both she and Zeus had been behaving a bit oddly all week, but this was *really* strange. Embarrassing, too!

"Wow! Your stepmom looks so different from the drawings of her in *Teen Scrollazine*," Pallas murmured to Athena.

"Younger," Eurynome observed.

It was true. Hera did look young, partly because she was acting like a little kid holding a doll. But also because her pretty blond hair was braided in three lopsided pigtails and she was barefoot! Zeus's hair was messy too. It was sticking up in disorderly spikes like he hadn't combed it in days.

"I know. It's weird. I just hope my dad remembered to bring my aegis. I'll need it for my competitions. Back in a sec," Athena told her friends.

She hurried over to the grown-ups. "Hi, Dad," she greeted him cheerfully. But Zeus gave no reply. He didn't even acknowledge her presence. He just kept crawling around while Hera kept giggling. Athena tried again. "Dad, did you remember my aegis?" When he still didn't pay her any attention, she tapped him on the shoulder as he crawled by.

Zzzt! "Ow!" She yanked her finger away. She'd gotten zapped by the sparks of electricity that rippled over his skin.

At her cry, Zeus finally leaped to his feet. "Theeny!" he crowed happily as if they hadn't seen each other for a year. He reached out and enfolded her in a big bear hug. *Zzzt!*

"Ow!" she squeaked as he accidentally zapped her again. Now that she was closer, she could see that he seemed to have lost the wrinkles at the corners of his eyes, and his hair and beard seemed a brighter red. Like Hera, he looked younger.

When he set her down at last, she stepped out of hugging reach and tried yet again. "Dad? Did you hear my question?"

Before Zeus could reply, Mr. Cyclops focused the single eyeball in the middle of his forehead on her.

"Questions? Are we playing a game? How about Simon Says? I like that one."

By now Hebe had finished drinking from her bottle and fallen asleep. Quickly Hera set her in the stroller that was parked under one of the olive trees. Then Hera looked at Zeus and Mr. Cyclops expectantly. "I love that game! I'll play! Can I start?"

The grown-ups gathered eagerly for the game, some of them clapping in excitement. Among them were normally serious types such as Mr. Eratosthenes, the school librarian, and Ms. ThreeGraces, the well-mannered Beauty-ology teacher. Athena frowned. They all wanted to play a little kid's game? Something strange was definitely going on here, but she didn't have time to get to the bottom of it right now.

"I'm in charge," Zeus boomed cheerily before Athena could ask about her aegis again. "*I'll* start

151

the game. And instead of 'Simon Says,' we'll call the game 'Zeus Commands.'"

He quickly tried to round up the dozen or so grown-ups. "Everybody line up!" he yelled. When nobody moved, Zeus roared even louder, "Do like I say!"

"You have to say 'Zeus commands' first," complained Mr. Cyclops.

"Oh, yeah. Zeus commands everybody to line up!" boomed Zeus.

As the grown-ups gleefully fumbled around to do as he'd ordered, Athena tried again. "But, Dad, what about my aegis? Did you bring it?" The aegis's magic wouldn't help her since magic was forbidden in the competition. However, it was her lucky shield, and considering how little she'd practiced and the fact that Zeus hadn't helped with that at all, she was going to need as much luck as she could get!

She'd caught his attention for the moment at least. Rubbing his bearded chin, Zeus glanced around. "Well, I brought it. Forgot where I put it, though. You'll have to look for it."

"Look for what? Is that a command?" the normally quiet-voiced Mr. Eratosthenes shouted. His eyes squinted at Zeus from behind his binocular-like glasses.

"No! It was not a command," Athena's dad yelled back. "Did I *say* 'Zeus commands'? I don't think so!"

"I don't like this game," Ms. ThreeGraces complained. "Can't we play a different one?"

Athena's eyes widened at her whining tone and the fact that she wore about a zillion necklaces, probably every single one she owned. Athena and Pallas used to do that, but only back when they were little and playing dress-up. Usually the Beauty-ology teacher spoke in an elegant, soothing voice, even when annoyed, so the whiny voice was not at all like her. And she had always looked stylish until now.

"No change-backs! I want to play this one," Hera grumped. And suddenly all the teachers were arguing over which game to play.

Giving up on them for now, Athena went over to the stroller to check on Hebe. The baby was sleeping quietly, with her pacifier in her mouth. Aww, she really did look sweet. So pink-cheeked and chubby. But just how she could sleep through all this commotion was a mystery.

Athena tiptoed around the stroller, looking for the aegis. However, she only spotted toys, bottles, blankies, and other baby stuff. Abandoning her search, she went back to her friends.

"No aegis?" Artemis asked, seeing Athena's empty hands.

"My dad brought it but forgot where he put it," she explained in frustration. "He just left it lying around somewhere, can you believe it? He knows that thing is important to me! Ever since Hebe came, he's been acting strange, and—"

"Who's Hebe?" Pallas interrupted.

"You haven't heard the news?" Artemis asked her in surprise. "It's only been plastered all over *Teen Scrollazine* and the *Greekly Weekly News* for a week now."

Pallas shrugged. "I've been too busy training lately to keep up with news."

"Same here," added Eurynome.

"Hebe is my new baby sister," Athena explained patiently. She had planned to tell Pallas about Hebe sooner. But then Pallas hadn't shown up or responded to her invitation, of course, which had kind of hurt Athena's feelings.

Pallas's jaw dropped. "You never told me your parents were having a baby!"

"I only found out a week ago myself. It was a 'magic' thing," Athena explained. When Pallas still looked confused, Athena and the other goddessgirls quickly told her and Eurynome the story of Hebe's magical birth.

"Whoa!" said Pallas afterward. "Getting a baby sister so unexpectedly like that must have come as a real shock. I'd feel like my world had been turned upside down if that had happened to me!" She gave Athena a sympathetic look.

Athena smiled at her old friend. Pallas under-stood *exactly* how she'd been feeling. "You nailed it. I'm starting to get used to it, but—"

Suddenly Zeus ran by. The grown-ups had moved on to a game of chase. Other teachers followed, all trying to tag him. Unfortunately for them, he shinnied up a cypress tree, as nimble as a monkey.

"Wow! Look at him go!" said Pallas, gaping.

"Is he always this energetic?" Eurynome asked.

"Well, not *this* energetic," said Athena, biting her lip. "I'm getting a little worried about him, but I'm not sure what to do."

The group watched in surprise as Muse Urania, MOA's Science-ology teacher, headed up the tree after Zeus. Meanwhile, the giant Mr. Cyclops began riding around the tree on a too-small tricycle with Hermes perched on his shoulders. Both were staring up at Zeus and Muse Urania and giggling like crazy.

"So I'm guessing this isn't normal behavior for MOA teachers?" asked Pallas.

"Far from it," Aphrodite answered. "And did you notice Hera's pigtails? Those are so *not* her."

"You don't suppose all this has to do with those youthful makeovers your Beauty-ology class was doing?" Athena asked her hopefully. It would be nice if the explanation were that simple. Maybe the makeovers were making the grown-ups feel temporarily peppy or something.

"Huh?" Aphrodite shook her head, sending her shiny golden hair swaying. "We haven't started that project yet. We're still practicing on those fake head models."

"Oh." Athena furrowed her brow as she studied the grown-up gods, goddesses, and mortals running amuck. Even if she'd known what to do about it, she really didn't have time to deal with this problem. She needed to be checking on things around the festival. And the competitions were set to begin soon!

"They're acting like little kids," Pallas murmured.

"It's almost like they're all under a spell or a curse or something," added Eurynome.

A spell or a curse? One that made grown-ups behave like little kids? But who would cast such a spell? Athena tried to puzzle it out. Suddenly she got an idea. "Do you think Hebe could have something to do with this?" she asked aloud. Three goddessgirls and two mortal ones looked at her in surprise.

"You think your adorable baby sister put a spell on the grown-ups?" Aphrodite asked, sounding doubtful.

Right then Hera came skipping by, hand in hand with the three-eyed owner of Cleo's Cosmetics. They paused to speak to the girls. "Cleo and I are going to do face-painting and hairdos for everyone in the art area! Come over if you want," Hera invited them. Both ladies giggled, then skipped down the path toward the art area together.

A puzzled look came over Artemis's face. "Hey, if Hera is off to do face-painting and Zeus just went up a tree, who's watching Hebe?"

They all looked toward the olive trees again, and Athena gasped. "No one, that's who!"

The six girls rushed as a group to stand in a circle around the baby's stroller. They breathed sighs of relief when they saw that Hebe was still sleeping peacefully, despite the chaos around her. As they watched, the baby stretched her little arms out of the blanket and opened her blue eyes.

"What kind of magic are you up to, little girl?" Athena wondered aloud.

But Hebe only cooed and gave them all a sweet, innocent smile.

9

Baby Trouble

Pallas

PALLAS GAZED AT THE PINK-CHEEKED BABY IN the stroller. So Athena had a new little sister. She was mega-cute! But was she also a spell-caster?

A gasp from Persephone caught Pallas's attention. "Ye gods! My mom's gone bonkers too!" she wailed. She was staring at a group of ladies dancing in a circle and singing "Ring around the rosie" farther down the path.

Persephone's mom, Demeter, was super-fond of plants and owned the flower shop in the IM. However, at the moment she was ripping the heads off a bouquet of flowers she held, as the others danced around her in a circle.

When they got to the part where they sang "We all fall down!" she tossed the flowers high into the air, to rain down on them. Destroying flowers didn't seem at all like something a flower-loving goddess like Demeter would do. Normally.

"I think I'd better take her home," said Persephone. She hurried over to her mom just as a teacher Pallas had met during her former visit to MOA came running past the olive trees from the art area. Her name was Ms. ThreeGraces. Seeing the girls gathered around the stroller, the teacher stopped. Her eyes sparkled and she bounced on her toes in excitement.

"Cleo painted my face and Hera styled my hair. Isn't it *kee-YOOT*?" Then, without waiting for a response, she skipped off.

The girls all stared at one another. Actually it looked like a clown had done the Beauty-ology teacher's makeup. Or a two-year-old. Her hair had been cut way too short in some places. And haphazard hunks tied with ribbons sprouted up in it here and there.

"I'd better get to the art area and oversee those makeovers before there are more disasters," Aphrodite announced. "Otherwise I'll probably spend the entire rest of the year doing makeovers of the makeovers to repair the damage!" With that, she dashed off.

With Aphrodite and Persephone gone, only four girls remained around the stroller. "What should we do about Hebe?" Athena asked, sounding worried.

About the baby being a spell-caster, did she mean? wondered Pallas. But Hebe was just an infant! So how could she be doing magic?

The baby was getting more active now, kicking her legs, waving her arms, and cooing like mad. "Uh, do any of us know how to take care of a baby?" Artemis asked. "I helped look after Apollo when we were little, but my mom was in charge."

"Eurynome and I do a lot of babysitting in Triton," Pallas assured her. Eurynome nodded from beside her.

"Yeah, I read that in your letters," Athena said to Pallas, sounding relieved.

The reminder of those unanswered letters caused Pallas's mood to plunge a little. It still hurt that Athena had only contacted her when she'd needed help. And Pallas suspected that she now knew the reason why Athena had wanted her help—because Hebe had appeared.

Suddenly a lyrebell sounded across the acropolis. *Ping! Ping! Ping!* The heads of the four girls swung toward the sound.

"Uh-oh, that's the herald. The reenactment competitions are starting," said Athena. "Good thing Coach Triathlon agreed to help organize them, 'cause Dad is useless as a grown-up right now." In fact, Zeus was still up a tree.

"Um, I don't think the coach is going to be much help either," said Artemis. "And what's Professor Ladon up to?" She pointed at a sandbox just past the trees, where a teacher with a whistle around his neck was happily building sandcastles that resembled gymnasiums. A dragonlike grown-up was sneaking up on him from behind.

Pallas figured the guy with the whistle must be the coach and the dragon-tail guy must be the professor.

Just then Professor Ladon yelled, "Sssurprissse!" With each *Sss* sound, he let out a blast of dragon fire that destroyed the castles the coach had built.

When the coach leaped up, he and the professor began yelling at each other and calling each other names. "Dragon lips! Pootie head!"

"You two! Stop that!" Athena called out to them. "You're responsible adults!" But this did no good. Professor Ladon zoomed off, with the coach after him, both name-calling all the while.

"I don't have time for this!" exclaimed Athena, sounding unusually frazzled. "I've got to go kick off the competitions at the arenas, plus check on everything else around here."

Artemis glanced at the scroll-filled helmet she still

held. "Some of the swordplay competitors haven't gotten their scrolls for the first bouts yet, but I'll take care of that at least." Athena sent her a grateful look.

As Artemis hurried off to the arenas, Athena peered down at the baby in the stroller, then up at Pallas. Her eyes were pleading when she said, "I don't know what to do about Hebe. Could you watch her?"

Pallas hesitated. She knew what Athena expected her to say and she couldn't let her down, but she was still smarting. Did Athena value her more as a babysitter than as a friend? Before she could decide how to reply, Eurynome spoke up. "I'll stay with the baby," she said.

"But you're in one of the first competitions!" Pallas exclaimed, aghast. "You should be reporting to arena A right now!"

Eurynome just shrugged. "It's okay."

"No, it's not," Pallas insisted. "You have to go. We trained hard for this!" Her mind made up, she turned toward Athena. "I'm not up till the second round, arena B. So I'll stay with Hebe until someone can come back and take my place."

"Are you sure?" asked Eurynome.

Pallas nodded. She wasn't going to let Eurynome sacrifice her chance to win the competition. That wasn't what true friends did.

"Thanks, Pal. I knew I could count on you!" said Athena. Then she and Eurynome dashed off.

Not long after they left, the baby began whimpering. Pallas offered her a finger to hold, but Hebe batted it away. Unfortunately, the pacifier was nowhere to be found in the stroller. Hebe's whimpering grew louder, and then she started to cry.

"Sorry about the pacifier. Would you like a toy

instead?" Pallas asked her sweetly. "I'll see if I can find one."

As she was searching among the baby things scattered around on a blanket on the ground, the baby's cries got louder and louder. "Whoa! You sure take after Zeus. He's loud too!"

Spotting a squeak toy, she plucked it from the blanket. Behind her the baby's crying stopped for some reason. "There, there," Pallas heard Athena say in a soft voice. "It's okay, Hebe. Everything will be all right."

Pallas jumped to her feet. "You came back!"

Athena looked over at her and smiled. "Mm-hm." She was holding her baby sister in her arms and rocking her gently.

"But what about the competitions?" Pallas asked. "I thought you needed to be at the acropolis to help organize. And aren't you competing too?"

"Not till later," said Athena. "I ran into Ares and Apollo on the way there. Their first bouts are later, too, so they'll help out with things for now."

"You didn't have to come back," said Pallas, handing her the squeak toy. "I could've taken care of Hebe by myself."

"I know," said Athena. "But what kind of friend would I be if I took advantage of your generosity? Besides, if we both look after her for a while, we'll get to visit with each other more!"

Any remaining doubts Pallas might have had about Athena's friendship crumbled to dust right then. Hebe gurgled, and Athena smiled down at her, showing her the toy. When Athena squeezed it, the toy squeaked and then spoke: "Every heart sings a song, incomplete, until another heart whispers back."

"That's Plato," Athena murmured to the baby. "Best writer ever. You're going to love him."

"Hebe's growing on you, isn't she?" Pallas said softly.

Athena looked up at her in surprise, then back down at the baby. "Yeah, I guess she is," she mused in a wondering tone.

"I could have told you she would," said Pallas. "You're going to be an awesome big sister."

"Think so?" asked Athena, sounding unsure.

"I *know* so," said Pallas. Athena excelled at everything she did, after all.

Hearing grown-up giggling in the distance, Pallas asked, "So do you really think there's some kind of curse or spell on your dad and the others? If there is, I don't see how Hebe could be responsible. She's just a baby."

"An *immortal* baby," Athena reminded her. "Who knows what powers she may have?"

Just then Hebe began to cry again. *Waa!* Athena cooed to her and rocked her more, but Hebe only cried harder. "What do you think is wrong?" Athena asked, sounding distressed. "She can't be hungry. Hera fed her a little while ago."

"I'll check her diaper," said Pallas. She slipped a hand inside the onesie the baby was wearing. "Nope, dry," she reported. "Thing is, babies cry an average of two hours a day."

"Really?" Athena said in surprise.

Pallas nodded. "I learned that in a class I took with Eurynome before we started babysitting together." It was fun to be the expert on the subject of babies. For once, she knew stuff the famous, amazing goddess-girl Athena didn't!

"What else can we try?" Athena asked desperately when Hebe kept on crying.

"Change the position you're holding her in," advised Pallas. "I couldn't find her pacifier, but I'll look again." As Pallas rummaged in the stroller for it, Athena shifted Hebe so she was holding her upright instead of sideways. Still, Hebe continued to wail. "Argh. Can't find it," Pallas said, giving up the search after a minute.

"Never mind," said Athena. "I just spotted it. Look!"

Pallas glanced up in time to see Muse Urania, who'd come down from the tree, go skipping by with the pacifier in her mouth. How and when the teacher had managed to grab it out of the stroller was a mystery. She popped it out just long enough to stop to take a drink from a three-tiered fountain at the edge of the olive grove, before merrily continuing down the path.

Waa! By now Hebe was crying at the top of her lungs.

"Hey, see that fountain? Let's wheel her over there," suggested Pallas. "Some babies are calmed by the sound of running water. Another tidbit I learned in that class."

"Good idea! Because that's actually Hebe's fountain, the one she magically appeared in. And Ms. Hydra, the office assistant, told me she likes hearing its water bubble." Athena set the wailing baby into her stroller, and together the girls pushed her close to the burbling fountain. Instantly the baby calmed, and her eyes closed drowsily. She was falling asleep again!

Athena flopped onto her back on the grass beside the stroller. "Thank godness!" she said with a relieved laugh. "Must be why my dad lugged that fountain here to the festival. He knew it would calm her."

Pallas flopped onto the grass alongside Athena. "Good thing he's strong. That fountain looks mega-heavy." Not only was the fountain three tiers tall, but it was also made of solid stone!

Just as the baby fell asleep, Eurynome returned. Her hair was untidy and she had a scuff on one shin guard. "Victory!" she called, punching a fist in the air.

Waa!

"Oops! Sorry," said Eurynome, putting a hand over her mouth. But it was too late. The baby was awake and crying again.

Ping! Ping! Ping! The lyrebell they'd heard earlier sounded once more. Pallas jumped to her feet. "I'd better go. Time for my reenactment in arena B!"

Eurynome had begun to gently jiggle the stroller, and already Hebe was quieting. "Good luck!" she and Athena wished Pallas in low, non-baby-waking voices as she dashed off.

Arriving just in time for her bout, Pallas saw that her opponent was a green girl with snakes for hair. Medusa! Today the girl wore eyeglasses. Thank godness for that, because as everyone knew, these special glasses prevented Medusa's gaze from turning other mortals like Pallas to stone.

The MOA herald struck his lyrebell with a little hammer. *Ping! Ping! Ping!* "Welcome to the battle of the Amazon Penthesilea versus the Greek hero Makhaon!" he told the crowd. "Meet the competitors!"

"I'm playing Penthesilea," Pallas called out, waving cheerily to the crowd.

"And I am to be Makhaon," Medusa announced,

taking a bow. All of her snakes bowed too, much to the amusement of Pallas and the audience.

The herald whipped out a scroll and read aloud to Pallas and Medusa the three rules of engagement. They were:

1. Swords are bespelled to prevent injury. Other than those spells, magic is not allowed.

2. If your opponent says "Stop," swords go down. Stop the bout immediately.

3. Competitors will accept the judges' declaration of the winner, to be based on the number of hits and fouls as well as crowd approval.

Turning to the audience, the herald reminded them in a loud voice that although the two contestants would be playing particular characters in an historic battle, either of them could win here. "So root for your favorite!" he called.

Everyone cheered. Many had probably come hoping certain battles *would* turn out differently today. For some people in the crowd, these battles were a chance to redeem a loss, which made the reenactments much more exciting and fun to watch.

At the end of this one, however, Pallas emerged victorious, the same as Penthesilea had in the original battle. It hadn't been easy. Medusa's snakes could be formidable, hissing and lunging to help defend the green girl. Not that Medusa needed help. Her offense was amazing, but Pallas saw an opening and scored just enough points to prevail.

When she went over to thank Medusa for the bout afterward, Pallas immediately noticed something amiss. One of the snakes on the green girl's head was drooping and looking cross-eyed.

"Ooh! Your poor snake. It looks dizzy!" Pallas exclaimed.

"Must have been the spin I did in my last maneuver." Medusa reached up to pet the droopy snake. "Sorry, Sweetpea," she told it.

"Yeah, that spin of yours was awesome. It really threw me off balance," Pallas agreed.

Athena had told her that Medusa had given names to all twelve of her snakes and considered them pets. And although this green girl had been mean to Athena earlier in the year, Pallas had been glad to read in one of Athena's letters a while back that they got along okay now.

Pandora came by a minute later, and Medusa took off with her to visit the arts and crafts booths. While

Pallas headed for her second match in the competition, she thought about Athena and Eurynome and hoped they were doing okay and having a good time taking care of Hebe. Her second bout turned out to be a reenactment of the battle of Ares versus the giant Mimon. A Titan boy named Epimetheus acted as Ares and was her opponent. She got the role of the giant!

In the real battle, Ares had won. But today Pallas was victorious. In a final maneuver that Achilles had taught her, she used some fancy footwork to throw Epimetheus off-balance as he thrust his sword toward her. It fell to the ground and so did he. Knowing she'd bested him, she *felt* like a giant!

Afterward, good sport that he was, Epimetheus came over to shake her hand. Then he left to find

Pandora and Medusa and hang out. Pallas recalled Athena saying something about an incident between Pandora and Epimetheus. It had involved some magical trouble bubbles that had ended with the pair crushing on each other. Apparently the crush was still in effect.

Pallas was hurrying off to her third bout when she passed Eurynome racing to get to her second one in a different arena.

"Athena just left for her first bout," Eurynome paused to tell Pallas.

"Baby report?" Pallas asked breathlessly.

Eurynome grinned. "All good. Persephone is back from seeing her mom home. So she and Aphrodite are taking care of Hebe. We fed and burped her and changed her diaper, and now she's sleeping."

Just then Athena was passing them, but she screeched to a halt to say hi. "I'm off to reenact Heracles versus the Nemean lion. I've got the role of Heracles. And Princess Urania, one of the daughters of King Pierus of Macedon, will play the 'lion' I'm battling. Wish me luck!"

"Good luck!" they all told each other. They hugged quickly, then dashed off in opposite directions. Pallas had a feeling the lion was going to lose in Athena's battle, just like it had in the real one!

As the sword contests proceeded throughout the day, all three girls continued to win their bouts and advance to higher-level competitions. Meanwhile, Athena's other goddessgirl friends took charge of Hebe.

After the third round, the field of sixty-four competitors had narrowed to eight, including

Pallas, Athena, and Eurynome. After the fourth round, only four competitors were left, but Pallas didn't know if Athena and Eurynome had made it through. It was time for their fifth preliminary bout. If Pallas succeeded in that round, she would be one of the two finalists. Fingers crossed!

10

Crossing Swords

Pallas

WOO-HOO! FILLED WITH JOY AND BRIMMING with new confidence, Pallas twirled and leaped her way to the Theatre of Dionysus below the acropolis. She'd won her fifth bout, which meant she had now made it to the sixth and most important bout: the finals!

Taking a chance that Hephaestus might finally

make an appearance at the highlight of the festival, she had stopped by the Triton chariot. Now her dad's crumpled sword rested in her cross-body bag, and she carried Achilles' sword Evgenís sheathed at her side. She was tired, but delighted to have made it this far in the competition. It suddenly seemed as though she actually had a shot at winning that grand prize sword!

Due to her detour to the chariot, the amphitheater was already packed with crowds when she arrived. She loped down one of the long aisles between the rows of bench seats, toward the stage. The seats at the front were made of gold-tinted marble. Wow! She spotted Artemis, Aphrodite, Persephone, Ares, Apollo, and other immortals in the audience. Including Zeus! He seemed to be behaving at the moment, though he was bouncing rather excitedly in his front-row seat.

Eurynome was there too, seated on the end of the first row with the baby stroller beside her and the fountain next to that. Athena must've asked someone to bring the fountain along to help keep the baby quiet. Probably Zeus or Heracles had moved it, since they were the strongest guys around. Anyway, Hebe wasn't making a peep, so the fountain was doing its job!

Pallas ran over to Eurynome and dropped off her bag. "I was hoping you'd make it to the finals too." She raised her eyebrows at her friend in question.

"Ares knocked me out of the running in the fourth round," Eurynome said, shrugging good-naturedly. "I'm just happy I made it as far as I did."

"Whoa! I bet he was a tough opponent," Pallas told her. Fortunately, she hadn't had to battle the godboy of war—so far.

Eurynome nodded. Standing up now, she angled the stroller so that Hebe was better shaded from the sun. "He was. I'm so glad *you* made it to the final, though. I wonder who you'll be up against. Not Ares, I hope."

"Ye gods, I hope not, too. Artemis wouldn't tell me the other finalist. They're trying to keep the suspense going as long as they can to make things more exciting for everyone." Pallas looked around the crowd. "So have you seen Hephaestus anywhere?"

When Eurynome shook her head, Pallas sighed. "Looks like he's not going to show."

"Maybe Athena can ask him about fixing the sword for you later," Eurynome encouraged. "Things will work out, don't worry."

Pallas nodded. She forced herself not to think too much about how disappointed her dad would be when she explained to him what had happened to his treasured old sword. Instead, she vowed to put all her brainpower and energy into this final bout.

"I'd better get down there," she said when she saw the herald stride onto the stage.

Eurynome hugged Pallas enthusiastically. "Good luck!" she said, holding up her necklace charm. Grinning, Pallas held hers up too, and they touched the *E* and the *P* together for extra luck.

A few seconds later, Pallas stepped onto the stage. Looking over her shoulder, she saw that Aphrodite and Persephone had joined Eurynome to help watch Hebe.

She still wasn't sure who her opponent would be. Though she knew there was a pretty good chance she'd be facing either Athena or Ares, it was still a shock when her BFF stepped onto the stage. And from the look on Athena's face, it seemed that she was feeling the same way.

"Hey, Pallas," said Athena.

"Hey, Athena." said Pallas. "Looks like we're the last two in the running."

"Mm-hm," said Athena. They wished each other a good match.

As the herald read the rules to the crowd, Achilles and Eurynome came up to the edge of the stage and waved Pallas over. "I know she's your friend, but don't let that throw you," Achilles advised.

"Remember, she's always busy with lots of responsibilities," Eurynome added. "She probably hasn't been practicing like you have."

Pallas looked over to see that Heracles, Artemis, Apollo, and Ares had called Athena over to the opposite edge of the stage to give her advice too.

"Hey!" Agamemnon called, running up. He beamed at Pallas. "So you made it all the way to the final bout? That's awesome!"

"Um, thanks. And isn't it great that Eurynome made it to the final eight?" Pallas replied. He hadn't even greeted Eurynome at all!

"Yeah, nice," said Agamemnon, barely glancing Eurynome's way.

Eurynome just rolled her eyes, having grown used to his rudeness. Then she returned Agamemnon's sword to him, since it had become clear she wouldn't win it.

As Agamemnon sheathed it, he said to Pallas, "Hey, maybe I could coach you from now on. Give you some pointers Achilles doesn't know. You could enter more contests and win stuff for me."

Pallas looked over at Achilles, expecting him to

speak up and protest, but he said nothing. Was he really going to chance letting Agamemnon steal her away as his pupil? *Hey! Wait a sec,* she thought suddenly. Maybe she could turn Agamemnon's offer to her advantage.

"Sure," she told him. "Let's switch now, okay? It'll be more official if I use *your* sword." She'd been doing just fine with Evgenís, the sword Achilles had lent her, but she knew that Achilles considered Briseis the better sword. And she was going to need the best one she could get if she was going to have any chance at beating Athena.

"Deal," said Agamemnon, without a moment's hesitation.

As Pallas returned the sword Evgenís to Achilles, he still said nothing. In fact, he wouldn't even *look* at her. She wished she could tell him why she'd made the bargain she had. But Agamemnon would hear.

"Okay! It's official. You're my champion now!" Agamemnon hooted when she took Briseis from him. He clapped Achilles on the back, acting cocky. "Sorry, dude."

Achilles just shrugged.

What was he thinking? Pallas wondered. That she was a traitor? If so, maybe it was a good thing he didn't speak up!

Ping! Ping! Ping! The Mount Olympus Academy herald struck his lyrebell. Then he called out from the stage in a loud, important voice, "Competitors, please take your places at the center of the stage."

"Get out there and slaughter her," Agamemnon encouraged Pallas.

Eurynome had her usual reaction to anything he said. She rolled her eyes. "Duh, the swords will be bespelled," she reminded him. "They can't injure each other."

Agamemnon ignored her. It was like she'd become invisible to him the minute she was out of the competition.

Despite whatever feelings Achilles might have about Pallas dumping him as a coach, he rallied enough to offer her some final encouraging words. "You can do this, Pallas. Just focus on the skills we practiced all week. And stay calm and cool."

"Easier said than done," said Pallas, her smile wobbling a little. Not wanting him to think her ungrateful, she added quickly, "Thanks for everything, Achilles." Then she turned away from her friends and let them retake their seats in the audience.

She and Athena went to stand on either side of the

herald, center stage. In a brief ceremony both girls'
swords were bespelled to prevent harm. Afterward,
Artemis came onstage. She presented the herald
with the helmet and then left again.

The herald showed the audience that the helmet
now held only two scrolls tied with matching baby-
blue ribbons. "Both scrolls display the name of the
same battle—the Trojan War. It remains only to see
which competitor will play which character."

He turned to Pallas and Athena and offered them
the helmet. They reached inside it at the same time
and drew out the scrolls that would decide their
assigned roles in this, the final bout.

Athena unrolled her scroll first. Surprise flickered
over her face. "I am to play the role of the Greek,
Achilles!" she announced as Pallas unrolled hers.

"And I am to be the Trojan, Hector!" Pallas

shouted. As the crowd cheered, she slid her eyes toward Achilles and gulped. What a huge coincidence that he would be one of the characters in this final bout! Still, they both knew how the original battle between these two had ended. Hector had lost and Achilles had won. Would history repeat itself?

Suddenly her confidence took a dive and doubt crept in. Back in Triton she and Athena had been fairly equal at wielding a blade. But what if Athena had only been going easy on her then, just to be nice? And how much *had* Athena been practicing since they'd last sparred?

As the enthusiastic whoops and clapping continued, Pallas watched Athena look over one shoulder at her fans. Of course Artemis, Aphrodite, and Persephone were cheering for her. Pallas didn't take it personally. They were Athena's best friends at MOA, after all.

Pallas looked over at her supporters one last time. Eurynome, Achilles, and Agamemnon punched their fists in the air. She smiled at them and took a deep, calming breath. This battle didn't have to turn out the way the original one had, she reminded herself. The outcome depended solely on how she and Athena played. It was up to her to do her best, win or lose.

She didn't really want to win if it meant there was a chance she would lose a friend, but what choice did she have? Athena wouldn't want Pallas to let her win on purpose, same as Pallas wouldn't want Athena to do that for her. She hoped for a fair victory. There was no guarantee that her dad's sword could or would be repaired, so she really needed to win a new one to replace it!

Just before the competition began, the herald told the audience one last thing. "This final bout will be decided a little differently from all previous bouts. You, the audience, will decide the winner this time. Display a thumbs-up for the winner you choose and a thumbs-down for the loser."

This brought huge applause. Over the sound, the herald went on, almost shouting to be heard, "Now, without further ado, let the battle begin!"

Athena and Pallas saluted each other with their swords. "On guard!"

197

11

Sportsmanship

Athena

ATHENA HAD KNOWN THERE WAS A GOOD possibility that she and Pallas would wind up pitted against each other in this final epic battle, but she'd hoped with all her might that it wouldn't happen. Just when they'd begun feeling close again like they had in Triton, now they were called upon to fight. But fight she would. Zeus was in the audience, and she wanted him to be mega-proud of her!

Once their bout began, she noticed that Pallas was a bit cautious in her parries and thrusts. Was she cutting Athena some slack because of their friendship? Athena hoped not. She wanted to win, but only in a fair-and-square contest. Pallas was talented. They'd been equally matched when they'd sparred back in Triton.

Athena's blade whooshed through the air, sometimes missing its target, but most often making contact with Pallas's sword in a loud *Clang!* "Good work," Pallas would compliment now and then. "Nice swing," Athena would say. They clashed over and over, each intent on scoring points.

Her own advantage as a goddessgirl was tempered by her rusty sword skills, making this an even match between her and Pallas. It was obvious that her childhood friend had been practicing regularly and learning new moves. Not only was she in the Cheer Blades, but rumor had it that Achilles—Athena's character in this battle, no less!—had been coaching Pallas. She was keeping Athena on her toes for sure!

As the competition went on, Athena sensed that Pallas's confidence was growing stronger. Her friend was obviously every bit as determined to win as Athena herself was. As Pallas lunged and swung her blade at Athena's chest, Athena really wished she had her lucky aegis to wear along with her armor. The aegis that Zeus had remembered to bring but then misplaced!

Athena parried, using one of the nine positions she'd been taught to protect the various parts of her body. Seeing an opening at last, she swung hard at Pallas.

Pallas parried, avoiding the blow. Then she pivoted her elbow, thrusting her blade with extra oomph toward Athena. But Athena saw it coming. Stepping back, she dodged the swinging blade and deflected it with her own.

On and on the bout went. Cheers and whoops sounded from the crowd now and then, as well as gasps whenever a hit was made. Trouble was, Athena and Pallas both knew each other's styles and moves. Neither got in very many good blows.

Suddenly Zeus's booming voice rang out from the audience. "Booooo, Pallas-Hector!" he called, shouting at Pallas from the stands. "Beat her, Athena-Achilles! Crush her like a bug!"

Finally her dad was paying attention to her again! Maybe Athena should've been pleased, but she wasn't. Because he was displaying really bad sportsmanship.

He was the King of the Gods and shouldn't take sides. Or boo her competitors. Especially not Pallas!

From the corner of her eye she noticed him jumping up and down excitedly like the child he seemed to have become lately. And he was waving something over his head. Her aegis! He'd found it after all!

12

New

Pallas

Booooo, PALLAS-HECTOR!" ZEUS SHOUTED AT Pallas from the stands. "Beat her, Athena-Achilles! Crush her like a bug!" he yelled.

Pallas didn't have time to dwell on Zeus's unsporting behavior. She was fighting the biggest battle of her life. And it was against her BFF!

However, Zeus was hard to ignore. Especially

since he was so loud! Whenever Pallas scored a point, he acted like a big bratty baby. "No fair. I want Theeny to win!" he'd say. Or "Pallas is cheating!"

Pallas could hardly believe what a bad sport he was being! Apparently Zeus had found Athena's aegis, because he was waving it around overhead now as he cheered Athena on.

Fortunately for Pallas, according to the rules, armor could not be changed mid-bout, so that aegis Athena considered so lucky wasn't going to help her.

She and Athena performed many leaps and flourishes, using their blades magnificently. Part of the contest was to put on a good show, after all. As the herald had said, the crowd would decide who would win. And each of them wanted that crucial thumbs-up!

Although both blades had been put under spells

to stop them from doing harm, it was still scary to have a sword come flashing toward you. Then, suddenly, something else came flying toward the stage from the audience. At first she thought it was a giant bird.

But no, it was Athena's aegis! Zeus had tossed it. That thing had magic powers, but Athena had only planned to wear it for luck. Still, it wasn't lucky for Athena that Zeus threw it! Her sword accidentally struck the aegis and got tangled up in it. Somehow, the magic of the aegis interfered with the spell that had been cast on Athena's blade to render it harmless. As her sword fell, it whacked Pallas's shoulder—hard.

"Ow!" yelled Pallas. The blow dropped her to the marble floor. To get out of harm's way, she purposely rolled toward the edge of the stage. Achilles rushed from his seat in the audience to make sure she was okay.

Meanwhile, up in the stands, Coach Triathlon had sneaked over to Professor Ladon, looking for some payback for the sandcastle incident. He reached over and pinched Professor Ladon's tail! The professor let out a blast of dragon breath. "You beassst!" he yelled. This set off an unforeseen chain reaction.

Thinking that a dangerous beast (such as a one-headed, two-armed, three-bodied, four-winged, six-legged Geryon) must have gotten loose in the theater, Apollo jumped up from his seat. In a single fluid movement he drew an arrow to his bow and took aim as he gazed around the theater, searching for the beast—his target.

At the same time, Professor Ladon's dragon fire happened to lick Zeus's back. "Yeeowch!" Zeus boomed. He leaped up, bumping into Apollo. Which caused Apollo to accidentally release his arrow just as Achilles leaped onstage, intending to go to Pallas's aid.

Boing! The arrow flew toward the stage.

"Ow!" yelled Achilles. He fell to his knees and then keeled over onstage in what appeared to be a dead faint.

Pallas, who hadn't been seriously injured by her fall, sprang to her feet and hurried over to kneel beside him. "Achilles? Achilles!"

Others, including Athena's goddessgirl friends, gathered onstage around them, murmuring in concern. "What happened?" "Is he okay?" "What's wrong with him?"

Instantly regretful, Apollo dropped his bow and also ran onto the stage. "Ye gods! I accidentally fired an arrow. I didn't mean to hit anyone. How bad is it?"

Pallas pointed at Apollo's arrow. "It struck Achilles' heel."

They shook Achilles' shoulder and yelled his name.

"It's only a flesh wound," said Apollo, sounding really worried. "It shouldn't have knocked him out like this."

"Think we should pull out the arrow?" asked Artemis. She and Apollo, who had some experience with such injuries, examined Achilles' heel closely.

"*Humph!* Achilles is always telling everyone how he's invincible because his mom dipped him in the River Styx," scoffed Agamemnon. "Not so much."

"Hush, you!" Pallas told him.

"Yeah, he's really hurt!" said Athena. "But Apollo's right. I don't get why Achilles isn't coming to."

"Oh no!" Pallas said, suddenly guessing what was

going on. "I'm sure Achilles was telling the truth that dunking him in the River Styx made him invincible. Most of him. Except where his mom's hand was holding onto him, though. His heel, I bet!"

"Because her hand would've been covering his skin there," said Athena, getting what Pallas was saying right away. "So his heel is the only place where he can still actually be wounded!"

"I'll handle this!" boomed Zeus, suddenly appearing onstage. Everyone backed off, letting him come to Achilles' aid. However, at the sight of blood, Zeus fainted too.

Ares, Poseidon, and Heracles gathered around Zeus, peering at him anxiously. "Suddenly he's scared of a little wound? What's wrong with him?" Ares wondered.

"He's been acting weird all day," said Heracles.

"I noticed that too. Acting like a little kid. And now a scaredy-cat!" said Poseidon, shaking his head in bewilderment.

Before anyone else could decide what to do next, Apollo gritted his teeth and pulled his arrow out of Achilles' heel. Everyone gasped. But still Achilles did not wake.

"Somebody get some water so we can see how bad the injury really is when the blood's been washed away," suggested Athena.

"I'll do it." Pallas flew into action. Spotting Mr. Cyclops's empty helmet on Artemis's seat, she leaped from the stage, grabbed it, and ran over to Hebe's fountain. Bending over its second tier, she scooped water into the helmet like it was a bowl. Then she rushed back to Achilles as fast as she could without spilling any water. Kneeling at his side again, she splashed the water onto his heel.

Gasps split the air, as to everyone's amazement, the skin around the wound instantly knit itself together, magically healing the injury. In mere seconds, Achilles revived and jumped up. "Wow! I feel great!" he announced, smiling.

Everyone stared at him in disbelief. "You're okay? Just like that?" asked Pallas.

"Better than okay. My feet feel amazing. I feel like dancing!" Since Agamemnon was standing next to him, Achilles grabbed the surprised boy's hands and led him around in a little jig.

"Hey, stop it, Dip!" demanded Agamemnon, yanking away. Achilles just laughed, as did the crowd gathered around him.

Athena looked at Pallas. "I wonder. . . does the water in that fountain have . . ."

". . . healing properties?" Pallas finished for her.

Athena nodded. "And we've seen grown-ups drinking from it. Muse Urania for one, remember? Plus I saw Hermes drink from it in my dad's office last Sunday."

Having caught on to where Athena's thinking was heading, Pallas brightened. "So maybe that's what's making the grown-ups act weird? The water? Maybe it's making them sort of . . ."

"*Kids* again!" she and Athena said at the exact same time.

Persephone's eyes went wide. "And that's probably why my mom was ripping up those flowers and acting so giggly?"

"I think so," said Athena. "Also the reason Ms.

Hydra was drawing on the walls when I went into her office last week. She must have drunk from the fountain!"

"And Zeus and Hera and our other teachers too?" asked Artemis. "It would explain how oddball they've been behaving." The students looked around at the grown-ups nearby. Most of them were either jumping up and down in their seats, or making faces at each other, or fighting.

"Hmm." Athena's brow furrowed in thought. Suddenly she gasped. "I just realized . . . I mean, I wonder if Hebe's fountain might be the legendary . . ."

"Fountain of Youth!" Athena and Pallas announced at the same time.

Everyone turned to look at them in surprise. "The what?" asked Aphrodite.

Athena quickly explained. "Back at my old school

on Earth, Pallas and I read a scrollbook by the Greek author Herodotus about a mythical Fountain of Youth. It was supposed to be a spring that turns back the clock. Those who are old and drink from it are made . . ."

". . . new again," finished Pallas. "Younger, in other words. In both looks *and* behavior. Which must be exactly what has been going on here." She and Athena grinned at each other. They'd begun to finish each other's sentences again, just like in the old days when Athena had lived in Triton.

All at once Pallas noticed a goddessgirl with short, spiky orange hair hovering nearby. Her ear was cocked toward them as she listened in. Athena noticed her too and looked a little worried. But before Athena could speak to her, the goddessgirl was gone with a flutter of her small, glittery orange wings. When Athena saw Pallas looking her way, she silently mouthed the girl's name: *Pheme*.

Uh-oh. Pheme was well known to be the goddess-girl of rumor and gossip. Whatever information she had overheard would soon be spread far and wide.

Pallas raised her eyebrows at Athena, silently asking what they should do about it, but Athena shrugged. There was nothing they could do.

"So you're saying the Fountain of Youth is *that* fountain?" said Artemis, drawing their attention. "And it's *real*, not mythical?"

"But why didn't its waters make *me* younger, then?" asked Achilles.

Everyone got quiet, thinking. Naturally, the brainy Athena was the first to come up with a plausible explanation. "Maybe because you didn't *drink* the water. It only touched your heel. Which watered down the effects, so to speak."

Murmurs of "that makes sense" ran through the students gathered onstage. As the others continued discussing the matter, Pallas got a wildly crazy hope-it-works idea. "I wonder what else it could make new." She ran over to her cross-body bag and pulled out her dad's ruined sword. Then she went over to the fountain and dipped the sword's blade into the bubbling waters falling from the second tier into the third.

Clank! Like magic the sword became straight and powerful again. Like brand new!

Pallas gasped, completely awestruck. She showed everyone the restored sword. "This must be what it looked like when my dad got it. All shiny and perfect."

Eurynome grinned at the sword, then at Pallas. "He's going to be so amazed!

"That's cool that the fountain works on both objects and living things," said Persephone. "And I'm guessing its effect on your sword will be permanent, since metal doesn't grow and change like people or plants do." She frowned. "But let's hope its effect on the grown-ups is only temporary. Because I want my *real* mom back."

Waa! Suddenly Hebe began to cry.

Athena hurried down from the stage and lifted the baby from her stroller. This time Hebe began to calm as soon as she was in her big sister's arms.

Athena smiled down at her, then up at all her friends. "Hebe says that she and I want our parents back the way they were too!" she announced, which made everyone laugh.

"But exactly how do we get the grown-ups to grow up again?" Aphrodite asked.

"We hide the fountain?" suggested Pallas. "And then hope they start to act more their ages?"

"Yeah, but what if they don't?" asked Eurynome.

Unfortunately, no one had a good answer for that.

13

Win or Lose

Pallas

S O WHO WON THE BOUT?" SOMEONE IN THE
audience called out.

"Good question." Artemis looked around at
the crowd. "What do you say? Who won the final
competition?"

In answer, about half of them jerked their thumbs

up for Athena and the other half for Pallas, which made it impossible to reach a decision.

"Guess the herald won't be much help breaking a tie," said Aphrodite, jerking her thumb over her shoulder. Pallas turned to see him riding away on Mr. Cyclops's tricycle, with the grand prize sword balanced over the top of the handlebars.

"Oh no! He must've drunk from the fountain during the sparring," said Eurynome.

"I say Pallas won!" Agamemnon shouted. "Zeus cheated when he threw that whatchamacallit aegis thing onto the stage, so Athena should be disqualified."

The audience began grumbling, some still favoring Athena as the winner and some favoring Pallas.

"Zeus should decide," Pallas suggested. "Later, when he's back to his grown-up self again, we can trust him to be sportsmanlike. He'll choose the person who won fair and square."

"Ha!" grumbled Agamemnon. "He's Athena's *dad*. He'll choose her no matter what."

Ignoring him, Pallas said firmly, "I trust him! We can count on Zeus."

"Whah? Did somebody call my name?" Finally recovering from his fainting spell, the King of the Gods sat up, looking woozy. Then he leaped to his feet. "What's going on here?" he demanded.

For half a second Pallas thought maybe he was back to normal. But then he grinned and said, "Who wants to play a game of Duck Duck Zeus?" After some other grown-ups in the stands responded excitedly that they were on board for that idea, they all ran off to begin.

Athena sighed, shaking her head at them. But then

her eyes lit with determination and she straightened up to gaze around at the remaining audience. "Before Apollo's arrow hit Achilles, Pallas had scored the most points," she said in a loud, clear voice. "And my dad did break the rules by interfering. Therefore, in my dad's place, I hereby award the win to Pallas!"

"I still think we should wait for Zeus to weigh in," Pallas argued. However, both girls knew she'd bested Athena, if only by a slim margin.

"No, take the grand prize. You're the winner," Agamemnon urged gleefully. He obviously couldn't wait to lay his paws on that bejeweled sword.

Pallas looked Athena in the eye. "Are you sure?"

Athena sent her a soft smile. "Absolutely, Pal." She went over and took the grand prize sword from the herald. Then she bestowed it to Pallas, saying, "Pallas, on behalf of Zeus, the King of the Gods and Ruler of the Heavens, I officially award you the grand prize in the Greek Fest competition!"

Seeing that the decision had been made, and that the two girls were in agreement about it, the crowd applauded politely and then began to exit the stands.

Pallas stared down at the sword's ruby-studded handle and its flashy blade. It truly was magnificent. She turned to Agamemnon. "Since you're my coach now, I believe this is yours." He started to grab it, but she held it back. "And in return you agree that I now own the sword I used in the final competition— Briseis? Fair trade?"

"Sure, no problem," he told her, his dazzled eyes on the prize.

"Okay, then." Pallas handed the prize sword to him. Then she picked up Briseis from where she'd dropped it earlier, and walked over to Achilles.

"Here you go. I'll trade you Briseis for Evgenís," she told him.

He took a step back, his expression stubborn. "You don't need to. I'm fine with keeping Evgenís, the sword I bought."

However, Pallas could see how his eyes gleamed at the sight of Briseis, and she knew how highly he valued it. After all, if she had won the far more valuable prize sword for him, instead of Agamemnon, Achilles himself had told her he planned to trade it to Agamemnon for Briseis.

"Both Mighty Fighty swords are the same to me," she told him. "I couldn't tell a bit of difference when I sparred with them." She stepped toward him again and spoke in a coaxing tone. "But you love Briseis best. So trade me."

Achilles' green eyes searched her brown ones.

Then he grinned, accepting that she'd meant what she'd said. "Okay, then. I will. Thanks!" After they made the trade, Pallas slid Evgenís into her scabbard. Achilles just stood there for a long moment, gazing at Briseis in his hands as if he could hardly believe his luck.

And for once Agamemnon didn't try to take what Achilles so clearly valued. He was too busy showing off the bejeweled prize sword to everyone who wanted a look at it.

Since Zeus and Hera weren't acting old enough (or at least *responsible* enough) to take care of Hebe for now, Athena invited both Pallas and Eurynome to sleep over in the dorms. "You can hang out and help me and the other goddessgirls take care of the baby," she suggested. "It'll be fun! C'mon, it's Saturday. No school tomorrow."

Eurynome shook her head. "Oh, I can't. Wish I could, but it's my little cousin's birthday tonight, and I promised I'd go to her party."

"How about you?" Athena asked Pallas.

"I can tell your parents if you want to stay," Eurynome promised Pallas. "If you think it'll be okay with them."

"They won't mind as long as they know where I am," said Pallas. She turned to Athena. "So that's a yes!"

The chariot carrying Eurynome and other villagers to Triton soon departed. Then Athena instructed Heracles to hide the Fountain of Youth in a secret vault within the Parthenon so that no one could ever again accidentally drink from it. Just to be extra safe, Pallas and Athena hung an OFF-LIMITS sign on it.

"Pallas!" Achilles came running over to her as the

girls came out of the temple. He drew her aside on the temple steps.

Beyond him Pallas could see Athena and some other girls bidding farewell to Persephone, who didn't live at the MOA dorm. Concerned about what kind of mischief her mom might have gotten into, Persephone was anxious to return to their house and check on her.

Apollo, Ares, and a bunch of their guy friends had already left. They'd made it their mission to see that all of the wacky grown-up immortals and mortals made it safely home.

"So, congratulations and all," Achilles told Pallas, drawing her attention. He looked away and then back at her. "Um, I was just wondering if, um, we could still maybe spar sometime, like maybe next week?"

A little thrill zinged through her at the thought of

hanging out with him again. She smiled at him, nodding. "Sure, sounds fun." After a moment's hesitation, she added, "I hope you know, I only agreed to have Agamemnon coach me because I wanted to use Briseis in that final bout. I knew you considered it the better sword. But regardless of whether or not it is, you are definitely the better coach!"

Her heart skipped a beat when he did that head-flick thing and smiled back. "Thanks. But next time we spar maybe you can teach *me* a thing or two, you Greek Fest reenactment winner, you!"

She laughed, and then he dashed off. His bud Agamemnon was proudly exhibiting his new sword to some mortal girls. He seemed to have forgotten all about coaching Pallas now that he'd gotten what he really wanted—that grand prize!

After Persephone departed, Aphrodite and

Artemis crowded together into Artemis's chariot, along with Hebe and her stroller. Pallas slipped her dad's now-gleaming sword back into her bag and slung its strap across her shoulder, while Athena tucked her aegis safely in with Hebe for the ride home. Then they all lifted off.

There hadn't been enough room in the chariot for Pallas and Athena, so they'd decided to fly alongside the chariot in winged sandals. Since mortals required the help of immortals to make such sandals work, Athena linked her arm through Pallas's and they all headed to MOA. It was Pallas's first time flying like this, but she caught on quickly and was soon balancing in the air like a pro.

"Hey! I should've said something before, but I want you to know I did read your last six letter-scrolls," Athena told Pallas a few minutes after they were airborne. "It's just that I got them late. Hermes only gave them to me this week."

"Oh," said Pallas. That explained it. She was really happy to learn there was a good reason why Athena hadn't responded to her recent letters.

"So from reading them, it sounds like you're having fun in Triton?" said Athena.

"Well . . ." Deciding that it was time to be truthful and clear the air between them, Pallas took a deep breath. "Everything's not quite as great as I made it sound," she admitted. "I didn't want you to feel sorry for me or think I couldn't have fun without you. I thought that if I made everything seem exciting in Triton, you might be more likely to come visit. It doesn't make sense, but that's what I was thinking. The truth is, I miss you like crazy."

"Really?" Athena brightened. "Me too! I never

told you, but when I left Triton for good that day, I was as terrified that you would make new friends without me as I was about starting a new school. I didn't realize till just now that ever since then, I've been assuming you'd be right there standing still in Triton and available whenever I need you. I didn't want you to change. I didn't want anything to change between us."

"But it has," Pallas said softly. "We don't get to hang out."

"Which stinks," said Athena. The wind turned momentarily fierce, so she banked left, in a move that took them both higher, where the air was calmer. Then she added, "You and Eurynome are friends, though, right?"

"Yeah, she's cool. Aphrodite and your friends are too."

"Yeah," said Athena.

Pallas debated whether she should spill her guts about her feelings and tell Athena that she was jealous of those girls being Athena's friends, but . . .

"I'm a little jealous," Athena announced meekly. Sounding slightly embarrassed, she told Pallas, "It's not an emotion I'm proud of—it seems unworthy of a goddessgirl—but I can't seem to help it."

"Me too," Pallas admitted, thinking that Athena meant she was jealous about Pallas's new friends the same way that Pallas was jealous of Athena's new friends.

"Why are you jealous?" Athena asked.

"Well, because . . . Why are you?"

"I'm jealous of Hebe. Because all of Zeus's and Hera's attention is on her now." She paused. "Or it *was*," she amended. Before they drank from the Fountain of Youth, she meant.

"Sibling rivalry," Pallas said, brushing her dark windblown hair from her face.

"Huh?"

"Happens a lot between the brothers and sisters I've babysat," Pallas told her. "I mean, like I said before, you've had practically zero time to get used to the idea of a baby sister." She shifted and leaned forward a little to keep herself balanced as they were buffeted by another air current. "Parents always focus on a new baby at first, so jealousy from an older sibling is understandable. It doesn't make you a bad goddessgirl."

Pallas turned her head toward Athena and locked eyes with her. "You could never, ever be a bad person," she said earnestly. "Just look at all the good stuff you do for mortals all the time. Like inventing the olive. Or holding the Greek Fest to build them a community center and gymnasium. You didn't have to do that."

Athena grew quiet, thinking. "Thanks. That helps a lot, Pal. But what did you mean before when you said you were jealous?"

"Oh, nothing," said Pallas, embarrassed to explain.

"C'mon," Athena coaxed. "I spilled my guts. Your turn."

For a few moments it got so quiet that they could hear the gentle flapping sound of the silver wings at the heels of their sandals. Pallas thought about Agamemnon and how he was always so jealous of what others had—especially Achilles—that he could never be truly happy. She didn't want to be that way.

So she took a deep breath and then admitted, "I

was jealous because you made so many friends so fast at MOA and because you wear that BFF necklace. But it's okay. I mean . . ."

Athena looked at her in surprise, then gestured toward the necklace Pallas wore. "But you've made friends too. When Hermes was flying me away to MOA, you were already walking to school with some other girls. I remember I felt like it was going to be easy for you to forget me."

"But you were the one going someplace new and exciting. I felt left behind." Pallas smiled and rolled her eyes. "Ye gods that sounds pathetic. I was happy for you that day too, though. Honest. You couldn't *not* go to MOA. Zeus commanded it. And you're, you know, a goddessgirl!"

"We need to find a way to hang out more. That's all there is to it!" said Athena.

235

"Yeah!" said Pallas. But exactly how they'd accomplish that, she wasn't sure.

Just then they broke through a cloud, and the Academy sprang into view up ahead. It gleamed in the sunlight atop the highest mountain in Greece.

"Wow," said Pallas. "I can hardly believe you live there!" The first time she'd been to MOA, she'd been whisked there by magic and so had missed this view!

Athena just laughed. "It's pretty much like Triton Junior High, actually. Only with magic and immortals and stuff." Which of course made Pallas laugh. Because those were things that made MOA *very* different from TJH!

After they touched down in the marble courtyard, they scurried up the Academy's wide granite steps with Aphrodite, Artemis, and Hebe to enter the school. They got dinner in the cafeteria first thing, and the eight-armed lunch lady filled several bottles with milk for the baby, while at the same time filling their plates. After dinner Pallas and Athena took the bottles with them and headed for the girls' dorm hall on the Academy's fourth floor.

Pandora was spending the night with her friend Medusa, which worked out kind of great. Because Pallas got to stay with Athena!

Most of the girls left their doors open up and down the hall and visited with each other all evening. They played games in the halls, had snacks, entertained Hebe, and hung out till late, having fun. But after a while more and more girls began to yawn, and doors along the hall began to close.

In Athena's room Pallas helped get Hebe settled into her stroller for the night. Then Athena and

Pallas snuggled in identical beds on opposite sides of the room. Even after they were in bed, they talked softly for a while. There was just so much to say! So they talked and talked till they were so tired that they finally drifted off to sleep. Zzzzz.

14

Headache

Athena

SUNDAY MORNING AFTER BREAKFAST ATHENA carried her baby sister to Zeus's office, walking with Pallas, Aphrodite, and Artemis. She had slipped a note under his door the night before so that he and Hera wouldn't worry if they snapped back to being their grown-up selves and discovered Hebe was gone.

On the way the girls joined up with Heracles and some godboys going there too. Concerned about Zeus, the boys announced that they wanted to make sure he was back to normal.

Hebe began crying the minute they all stepped inside the office together. Immediately, Zeus opened his arms wide. "Hand her over," he commanded. "She likes my singing."

Huh? When Athena passed Hebe to her dad, he took a deep breath and opened his mouth. She braced herself for what she knew was coming. She had heard him sing before. And although he had many, many talents, singing wasn't one of them.

> *"Rock-a-bye, Heebee*
>
> *In the treetops . . ."*

As Zeus belted out a lullaby off-key, the students cringed. A couple of boys actually held their ears. But amazingly, her dad's claim turned out to be true. Hebe was the one person in the office who appreciated his singing. She immediately stopped crying and began to gurgle happily.

"How's my wuvwee widdle thunderbolt?" Zeus cooed to her after he'd finished his song. "Dancey wancey woo!" As he whirled her in an impromptu dance around his messy office, Hera came in. Her pigtails were gone, and she looked more put together than she had over the past few days, which Athena took as a good sign. Smiling at Zeus and Hebe, Hera joined in their dance.

"Oh no! Zeus and Hera are still acting weird," murmured Ares.

"When other realms find out what's happened to Zeus and most of our teachers, MOA will be a laughingstock," Apollo wailed quietly.

"It's so embarrassing," said Poseidon, shaking his head.

"No, it's not," Athena said, coming to her dad's defense. "Besides, they *are* their grown-up selves again," she added, though she wasn't quite a hundred percent certain of this. Hebe looked so tiny in Zeus's big arms as he spun her around the room that Athena's heart melted for both of them.

"There's nothing cuter than dads taking care of their kids," Aphrodite added, sighing happily at the sight.

The other girls nodded.

"Yeah, Zeus and that baby are adorable together," Heracles pronounced. All the students turned to look at him in surprise. Especially the boys. Athena wasn't sure that she'd ever heard the word "adorable" pass the lips of a boy before unless it was said with sarcasm. Which definitely wasn't the case here. It only made her like Heracles more.

"What?" Heracles looked confused by the fact that everyone was staring at him.

"Bravo! Well said," Pallas told him, clapping. Athena beamed at her, glad to see that her mortal friend approved of her crush.

Aphrodite and Artemis nodded approvingly too.

After Hera took the baby off for a nap, Athena peered closely at her dad. "So you're back to normal, right?"

Zeus's eyebrows slammed together. "What do you mean? Why has everyone been asking me that all morning?"

"Uh, nothing. No reason. Just glad you're feeling okay," Athena told him. If Zeus didn't remember his silly actions of the day before, it was best not to remind him. Hera had seemed okay too. Athena breathed a sigh of relief that the fountain's effects apparently wore off quickly once a person stopped drinking its water.

"Only thing is, my sandals are full of sand and my knees are all scraped up for some reason," Zeus admitted.

Recalling his tree-climbing and crawling activities from yesterday, Athena could imagine why that was. However, since she and the other three girls could tell he was back to himself now, they wisely said nothing. The boys watched Zeus closely, though, still seeming suspicious as to whether he was totally, one hundred percent normal again.

"So, congratulations, Theeny!" Zeus roared abruptly.

Athena blinked at him. Did he mistakenly think she'd won the sword reenactment?

"I heard what happened," he went on. "That you awarded the grand prize in the final competition to your friend Pallas when I was, uh, taking a nap or something." He looked a little confused for a second, as if he'd actually remembered a bit of what had happened yesterday. But then he shook off his confusion.

"And you agree with my decision?" asked Athena, relaxing.

"You betcha!" He glanced from her to Pallas. "From what I remember, your friend scored more points."

His gaze swung back to Athena. "Immortals like us live for the pursuit of excellence in all things, so the fact that you awarded the prize to Pallas and ruled against yourself in such a noble way showed true *valor*! It was the right thing to do. I couldn't be more proud of you!" he boomed.

Athena was so delighted that she didn't even mind that he zapped her a little when he unexpectedly swooped her into a hug.

Finally seeming convinced that Zeus was back to being a grown-up again, the boys all left the office for a javelin game on the MOA sports fields. Maybe finding out that a strong heroic guy like Heracles approved of a dad going gaga over a baby would change their attitudes, mused Athena, watching them go. She hoped so, anyway.

"Now, I just have one question," said Zeus, drawing her gaze again. "Where's that fountain?"

Athena and her three friends glanced at each

other with wide eyes. Had he recalled everything after all?

"Athena thought it best to leave it at the acropolis," Aphrodite volunteered.

"Another excellent decision," Zeus told Athena. "Because I've decided to make that fountain an altar to your little sister."

"In *my* temple?" asked Athena, unsure she liked that idea.

"No! Once the new Cynosarges Center is built for the people of Athens, Hebe's fountain will stand *there* as an altar where mortals can worship her and bring gifts. What do you think?"

"Well . . . ," began Athena. She needed to tell him the truth about that fountain, about what its waters could do.

"If you're worried about her fountain being the

Fountain of Youth, fear not," he said, surprising them all. "As long as Hebe isn't anywhere near it, I'm certain its waters will lose their powers."

"How—," Pallas began.

"How did I know?" he boomed, finishing her sentence. "I'm King of the Gods and Ruler of the Heavens. I know everything! And anyway, Pheme told me about the fountain's magic first thing this morning. Plus I consulted a few ancient scrollbooks to determine the extent of its powers myself."

Aha! Athena and Pallas shared a look. They'd both seen Pheme listening in on their conversation the day before. Apparently that gossipy girl had told Zeus what she'd overheard. But in this case, her gossip-spreading had helped matters rather than cause trouble. You never knew which it would be with that girl.

Athena smiled. "Your altar idea sounds perfect!"

"Yeah! Great idea!" Pallas said enthusiatically.

"Fabulous," said Aphrodite, and Artemis nodded.

At their approval, Zeus beamed.

Just then Ms. Hydra's impatient purple head ducked into Zeus's office. "A chariot has arrived for Pallas of Triton," it announced before withdrawing.

Athena looked at Pallas in dismay. "Oh no! I was hoping we'd have a little more time before Hermes came for you." Her heart squeezed at the thought of losing Pallas again so soon.

"Me too," said Pallas, looking crestfallen.

As they walked down the hall, Athena's mind was racing. "Hey, I was just thinking that there could be a way that we can hang out more from now on," she said as they neared the Academy's bronze front doors. "Especially since you know a lot of stuff about babies from all your babysitting."

Pallas sent her a hopeful look. "Yeah?"

Athena nodded. "Stay here. I'm going to race back to my dad's office and ask him if you can come visit to give everybody baby care lessons and help me babysit Hebe once a week or something. That way, he and Hera can have like a date night—time to themselves. Would you want to?"

"Are you kidding?" said Pallas. "That would be awesome! Maybe you'd better wear your lucky aegis when you ask, though."

Athena grinned. "I'll chance it on my own. Just tell Hermes to wait, okay? I'll be right back." With that, she turned and practically flew back down the hall to Zeus's office.

He was at his desk when she went in. Since she was without her aegis, she decided to cross her fingers behind her back as she quickly outlined her baby-sitting proposal. Zeus didn't even hesitate before replying. "Excellent idea, Theeny. I like your level-headed mortal friend. And Hera and I could use a night out every now and then."

Athena was surprised at how easy it had been to convince him!

He smiled at her, his eyes twinkling. "So is that all, my favorite daughter in the whole wide world?" There was a pause, and then he added, "Guess I'd better make that my favorite *older* daughter."

She wasn't sure how she felt about him having *two* favorite daughters. But then her mind went to another related matter. "So, Dad? There's something that's been bugging me. A few days ago I heard you say I used to give you headaches. I knew my mom gave you headaches, since she was a fly buzzing in your head and all. But was I really such a pain?"

Zeus's brow wrinkled in confusion momentarily, and then he laughed. "Oh, that! I was referring to the manner of your birth. You popped out of my head, remember? And until you got out, you did give me terrible headaches for a while!

"But I'd do it all over again, because you were definitely worth the pain." He leaned forward to smile at her as he tapped a fingertip to the side of his head. "And besides, I figure you inherited my brains by being in there. That must be why you're so smart. You take after me!"

"Totally," Athena agreed, smiling at him.

As she dashed off to the courtyard to meet Pallas, she decided it would be okay for her dad to have more than one favorite daughter. Just like she could have more than one BFF. There were no limits to the amount of love one person could have, after all. A person could always find room in their heart for more.

She burst out of MOA's front doors just in time to see Hermes' chariot lifting off from the courtyard with Pallas inside, seated among a bunch of packages. *Oh no!* Pallas must not have been able to convince him to wait. That Hermes was always in such a hurry!

Athena wished there had been time to tell Pallas about her talk with Zeus. Instead she could only call up to her, "Bye! I'll miss you! Talk soon!"

"Bye! Okay!" Pallas called back.

Athena waved at the chariot till Pallas was out of sight, just like Pallas had done that day when Athena had left Triton. She could now kind of understand how hard it must have been for her friend when she'd left. Because though Pallas had only just now departed MOA, Athena could hardly wait to see her again. And with any luck, that day would come soon!

15

Silver and Gold

Pallas

"ON GUARD!" *CLANK! CLANK!*

It was the following Thursday after school, and Pallas and Eurynome were practicing on the Triton Junior High athletic field. Pallas wielded the sword Achilles had traded her for Briseis. She was pleased to have her very own sword at last and had decided to keep the name Agamemnon had given it, Evgenís—

seeing as how it truly was a fabulous and noble sword!

When she'd returned her dad's treasured sword to him in brand-new condition, he'd actually shed a tear. And though he'd wanted her to go on using it, he'd understood when she'd preferred to use a sword she had truly earned.

"That new sword of yours got you to the final competition, so I can see why it's special to you. In all honesty, I think our swords choose *us*," he'd told her.

Clank! Pallas made a particularly amazing move on the field right then, whirling around backward before striking with her blade. Eurynome paused to applaud. "Woo-hoo! Good one, BFF!"

BFF? Is that what they were now? Pallas wasn't sure how to respond. Before she could think more about it, a messagescroll arrived from MOA from Athena! Pallas caught it in midair.

Inside it she found a bracelet that touched her heart. A silver charm hung from it, formed into the entwined letters *P* and *A*, for "Pallas" and "Athena." Athena explained in her letter that she had had Hephaestus make each of them identical charms in his forge. Engraved on the back of both were these same words:

We've made new friends,

But we honor the old.

In the rest of the poem, old friends were the gold friends, and new friends were the silver ones. Since the charms were silver, maybe Athena had gotten the silver and gold friends mixed up. But who cared? And besides, you *could* say the two of them were actually *new* old friends, since they'd only recently re*new*ed their friendship. And now that friendship was stronger than ever.

There was a drawing of Athena on the back of her letter, wearing her usual gold *GG* charm necklace. But now there was also a silver *P* and *A* charm on the bracelet at her wrist, identical to the bracelet she'd sent Pallas.

"It's so cute! Here, let me help you clasp it," said Eurynome. Pallas held out her wrist, and Eurynome did just that. They both gazed at it admiringly for a moment. Then Pallas read the rest of Athena's letter aloud:

"My dad agreed that you can come to MOA one afternoon a week to teach a class in babysitting for anyone who wants to take it. And you can sleep over if your parents say it's okay. (Hope they do!)

One last thing, Pal. To celebrate our friendship and show everyone how important you are to me, I've placed a statue of you called a Palladium in my temple as well."

"Wow! What an honor," said Eurynome. Then, looking a little anxious, she said, "I know you're BFFs with Athena. Was it okay that I called you my BFF a while ago? If you don't want me to, I'll understand. I—"

"Wait! Stop!" said Pallas, shushing her. She tucked Athena's letterscroll into the pocket of her chiton. Then she briefly touched the *P* charm on her necklace to the *E* charm Eurynome wore. Catching her friend's gaze, she said firmly, "We are absolutely, most definitely BFFs. We can be *M*BFFs, as in 'Mortal BFFs,' and Athena can be my *GG*BFF!"

A smile that matched Pallas's own spread across

Eurynome's face. "Perfect!" she said. Then they both jumped around, and even did a couple of cartwheels, feeling and acting silly with happiness. Pallas felt *doubly* happy, in fact. Because now she had two BFFs!

Over time she felt certain that she would be able to open her mind and heart to other new friends as well. Meanwhile, with Eurynome as her MBFF and Athena as her GGBFF, her double friendships were sure to bring her *twice* the joy!

Looking for another great book?
Find it
IN THE MIDDLE.

Fun, fantastic books for kids in the in-beTWEEN age.

IntheMiddleBooks.com

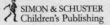

Did you LOVE reading this book?

Visit the Whyville...

IN THE MIDDLE BOOK HIVE

Where you can:

- ⬡ Discover great books!
- ⬡ Meet new friends!
- ⬡ Read exclusive sneak peeks and more!

Log on to visit now!
bookhive.whyville.net

Whyville